Elizabeth Ferrars and The Murder Room

>>> This title is part of The Murder Room, our series dedicated to making available out-of-print or hard-to-find titles by classic crime writers.

Crime fiction has always held up a mirror to society. The Victorians were fascinated by sensational murder and the emerging science of detection; now we are obsessed with the forensic detail of violent death. And no other genre has so captivated and enthralled readers.

Vast troves of classic crime writing have for a long time been unavailable to all but the most dedicated frequenters of second-hand bookshops. The advent of digital publishing means that we are now able to bring you the backlists of a huge range of titles by classic and contemporary crime writers, some of which have been out of print for decades.

From the genteel amateur private eyes of the Golden Age and the femmes fatales of pulp fiction, to the morally ambiguous hard-boiled detectives of mid twentieth-century America and their descendants who walk our twenty-first century streets, The Murder Room has it all. **>>>**

The Murder Room
Where Criminal Minds Meet

themurderroom.com

Elizabeth Ferrars (1907–1995)

One of the most distinguished crime writers of her generation, Elizabeth Ferrars was born Morna Doris MacTaggart in Rangoon and came to Britain at the age of six. She was a pupil at Bedales school between 1918 and 1924, studied journalism at London University and published her first crime novel, *Give a Corpse a Bad Name*, in 1940, the year that she met her second husband, academic Robert Brown. Highly praised by critics, her brand of intelligent, gripping mysteries was also beloved by readers. She wrote over seventy novels and was also published (as E. X. Ferrars) in the States, where she was equally popular. *Ellery Queen Mystery Magazine* described her as 'the writer who may be the closest of all to Christie in style, plotting and general milieu', and the *Washington Post* called her 'a consummate professional in clever plotting, characterization and atmosphere'. She was a founding member of the Crime Writers Association, who, in the early 1980s, gave her a lifetime achievement award.

By Elizabeth Ferrars
(published in The Murder Room)

Toby Dyke
Murder of a Suicide (1941)
 aka *Death in Botanist's Bay*

Police Chief Raposo
Skeleton Staff (1969)
Witness Before the Fact (1979)

Superintendent Ditteridge
A Stranger and Afraid (1971)
Breath of Suspicion (1972)
Alive and Dead (1974)

Virginia Freer
Last Will and Testament (1978)
Frog in the Throat (1980)
I Met Murder (1985)
Beware of the Dog (1992)

Andrew Basnett
The Crime and the Crystal (1985)
The Other Devil's Name (1986)
A Murder Too Many (1988)
A Hobby of Murder (1994)
A Choice of Evils (1995)

Other novels
The Clock That Wouldn't
 Stop (1952)

Murder in Time (1953)
The Lying Voices (1954)
Enough to Kill a Horse (1955)
Murder Moves In (1956)
 aka *Kill or Cure*
We Haven't Seen Her Lately
 (1956)
 aka *Always Say Die*
Furnished for Murder (1957)
Unreasonable Doubt (1958)
 aka *Count the Cost*
Fear the Light (1960)
Sleeping Dogs (1960)
The Doubly Dead (1963)
A Legal Fiction (1964)
 aka *The Decayed Gentlewoman*
Ninth Life (1965)
No Peace for the Wicked (1966)
The Swaying Pillars (1968)
Hanged Man's House (1974)
The Cup and the Lip (1975)
Experiment with Death (1981)
Skeleton in Search of a
 Cupboard (1982)
Seeing is Believing (1994)
A Thief in the Night (1995)

Sleeping Dogs

Elizabeth Ferrars

An Orion book

Copyright © Peter MacTaggart 1960

The right of Elizabeth Ferrars to be identified as the author of this work has been asserted in accordance with the Copyright, Designs and Patents Act 1988.

This edition published by
The Orion Publishing Group Ltd
Orion House
5 Upper St Martin's Lane
London WC2H 9EA

An Hachette UK company
A CIP catalogue record for this book is available from the British Library

ISBN 978 1 4719 0710 4

www.orionbooks.co.uk

CHAPTER ONE

At last the thin, self-pitying voice in the other room stopped for good. It had often stopped during the last few days. There had been long pauses and we had hoped, my half sister Janet and I, that that was the end. But then the voice had started again, always on that soft, excruciating note of complaint. It had got more and more on my nerves and I had gone out as much as I could and made Janet come out, too. But she could not really go out a great deal and did not like being left alone either. So, as I was there mainly to keep her company and to try to keep her in a confident state of mind, I had had to spend most of my time in the small basement flat, or in the pocket handkerchief of sooty garden outside it, listening to the voice of a woman whom, without my ever having set eyes on her, or heard distinctly more than a few words of all that she had said to my brother-in-law, Bernard, I had almost come to hate.

It was the monotony of her self-pity that had done it. I knew more or less what she had been through during the last five years and that she had reason to be sorry for herself, and if only she had sometimes

1

been angry and just sometimes amused, I think I should have managed to feel sorry for her. As it was, by the time that that final silence came, I was prepared to believe that she deserved everything that had happened to her.

Janet realised as soon as I did that this was the end. There had been a change of tone in the last sentence and Bernard had also spoken a little, which he did very rarely. Then all at once he had given a loud, exuberant whistle.

Janet lowered her knitting into her lap, looked across the room at me, and smiled.

"That's it, at last," she said. "It's been worse than they usually are."

I had taken to knitting, too, because reading had been impossible. I threw the rather tangled-looking job aside now and stood up and stretched.

"I don't know how you stand it," I said. "Or how Bernard does either."

"There's money in it, and we always need money," Janet said.

"Well, shall I get tea now?"

"That'd be lovely. Bernard will be out in a few minutes, I expect."

"But this isn't the actual end of the job, is it?" I said.

"Oh no, there's still a lot to do. But the tough part's over now. He doesn't mind the rest of it."

Her needles started clicking again. She knitted with the angry concentration of the nervous, her lips bitten and her forehead in tight wrinkles.

She was knitting a vest for the coming baby, which was due in a month now. After a bad beginning, she was keeping pretty well, but she could not really believe this of herself. She was thirty-eight, had been married for fourteen years, and this was the first time that she had even become pregnant. The extremity of her own longing and Bernard's was a burden that her nerves could not carry, and in her heart she was agonisingly convinced of disaster and loss. I had been finding her very difficult to handle, though she tried hard not to be.

Going out to the kitchen, I put the kettle on the gas stove and three cups and saucers on a tray. Bernard liked a big tea, so I buttered some scones and took the Dundee cake and chocolate biscuits out of the cake tin, putting them all together on one plate. The cake came from the baker at the corner and tasted like sweetened sawdust. Cooking, however—and particularly baking—is an art that I have not acquired. But Bernard and Janet had been very patient about the things that I had been making them eat. I made the tea and took the tray into the sitting room.

It was a fair-sized room, which had been the kitchen of the big Hampstead house in the days before it had been divided into flats, and except that the two windows were rather small and gave a view only of the feet and ankles of the people who went by on the pavement above, it was a pleasant place. In the days when it had still been hard for Janet to find enough to do to use up her energy, she had painted each wall a different colour and had stuck a dark blue paper, with a pattern of gold stars, on the ceiling. There were a few good pieces of furniture from our old home; some lithographs of very abstract paintings; some comfortable, battered chairs; a gas fire; a lot of books; a radio-recordplayer; an old treadle sewing machine; and the divan on which I had been sleeping. Janet had painted the walls of the small area outside the windows white and had stood a couple of bay trees in green pots in its corners. Considering how little money there had been, it was a creditable effort.

She looked now at my idea of a presentable tea tray and gave me a smile which said both thank you and that I was hopeless and we all knew that it could not be helped. She was pallid and looked tired. Her crinkly fair hair, which already had a few streaks of grey in it, hung wispily about her face, from being clawed at by her short, strong fingers. Her grey eyes had blue-black smudges under them. She was wearing a flowered smock, a cotton skirt, no stockings, and red espadrilles that dated from last year's holiday in France.

She was a small woman and normally was slim and bothered a great deal about how she dressed. She was fifteen years older than I was, and I suppose because she had been more or less grown-up for as long as I could remember, I had never really noticed any changes in her until the last few months. Those changes had put me into a troubled and protective state of mind, to which neither of us was accustomed.

Putting the tea tray down on a low table beside her, I went to a door in a corner of the room, which led into what had once been the pantry, knocked and called out, "Tea, Bernard!"

He did not answer and it was almost ten minutes before he came out to join us. Janet was fretting because his tea would be cold, but when I offered to make some more, he shook his head, remarked that he liked his tea cold, rubbed his hands together gleefully, and said, "And that's that, my dears! Everything over bar the shouting. And that won't take me long now. I know just how I'm going to handle it."

His voice was hoarse with a cold that had been threatening for a day or two and his eyes were red and watery. He was forty-five, tall and thin, and as he settled into one of the low armchairs, he seemed to be all long, untidy arms and legs, knotted up in a queer bundle. He had wiry brown hair with a tinge of red in it, which he ought to have had cut more often than he did. His eyes were wide-spaced, a clear blue, and with a slight cast in one of them, which gave him an impish, equivocal expression.

"You can leave the rest till tomorrow," Janet said to him, "and go to bed early for once. You'll work all the better for a break."

That was something that she had been trying to make him believe for fourteen years, but once Bernard started a job of work, he went on, day and night almost, until it was finished. He did not really believe that any other way of working was possible and did not know what the phrase "regular hours" meant. During the last week I had sometimes heard him come tiptoeing out of his little room, trying not to wake me as he crept by on his way to bed, at three in the morning.

"Ah, I'm almost done, almost done," he answered, rubbing his bony hands together again and making the knuckles crack. "If I keep at it now, I'll be finished by tomorrow. And that'll be money in the bank, which is something we can do with. And also I'll have the damn thing off my mind and be able to enjoy a rest. I've decided that when I'm paid I'm going to give myself one treat. I'm going to buy a record of *Tricorne*. And you can have the rest, Janet, every last penny of it, for safekeeping. What about that?"

"Your cold's worse," she said. "Your voice sounds much thicker. D'you think you've a temperature?"

"I feel fine," he answered. "I know just how I'm going to finish the job, and that's a grand feeling. Ah, she was a find, that woman. An incredible piece of luck, just when we needed it."

I looked at him with a sudden feeling of distaste. "You sound as if you've been *enjoying* it."

He turned his bright blue, ambiguous gaze on me.

"Three quarters of the time, on this sort of job, I feel quite simply sick," he said. "But there's always a time towards the end—probably it's when I begin to hear the crackle of that cheque in the offing— when the fascination of the thing begins to get me. The people themselves begin to seem amazingly interesting. I begin to feel I know them. And I begin to feel I have a sort of power over them. As I have, of course—I'm a very important man to them for a little while. And this woman particularly. There was something about her. . . ."

"D'you think she *was* innocent?" Janet asked. Her voice was strained. I knew that this question had been on her mind all the time that she had had to sit listening to the voice next door. "Now that you think you know her—did she or didn't she murder that child?"

It was its having been a child, of course, that had affected her so much. I thought that Bernard might have thought of that before making his arrangements with Teresa Swale. But he had only been able to think of the money to be made out of her.

Through a mouthful of Dundee cake he answered, "I'm actually far less sure about that than I was before I started. If you'd asked me that at the beginning, I'd have said oh yes, of course she's innocent, poor woman. The victim of circumstances. She was acquitted, wasn't she? And she was acquitted because there really wasn't any evidence against her. And the way suspicion's dogged her ever since is sheer wickedness, a thing that ought to be shown up and denounced for the abominable injustice it is. But now . . ." He had a fit of coughing, blew his nose wetly into a paper handkerchief, and went on, "Somehow I now think it's she herself who created a good deal of the suspicion. She always protested her innocence so much. She simply wouldn't get her mind off it and talk about anything else. She kept telling me over and over again about her wonderful character and how nothing had ever been said against it before. Yet half the time I was expecting her to slip a hand in my pocket when I wasn't looking and steal my wallet. Not that she ever did—so I was being entirely unjust myself. But there was something about her that put that sort of idea into my mind. No, I really don't know what I think now. I suppose she's innocent. She probably is. Anyway, it's more comfortable to think so."

"Well, I think you've discovered an appallingly morbid way of earning a living," I said. "If I were Janet, I shouldn't allow it."

"Listen to darling Elspeth, who hasn't even drawn her first salary cheque yet," Bernard said good-humouredly. "The time can come when you'll be quite happy to earn money where you can find it."

I knew theoretically that this was true. I even knew that the time he spoke of might not be so very far ahead, because I had a feeling that the career that I had chosen might not be as attractive as a number of people had tried to persuade me that it would be. I had been restive about it for some time. But I had gone through university on a grant that had been given to me on condition that I ended up by becoming a teacher, a condition that I had accepted while I was still too young to know better. And a teacher in an enormous girls' school near Nottingham I was about to become in September.

Some sense of obligation made me feel that I should have to stick to it for at least a year or two, if only to prove to other people what an extraordinarily bad teacher I was bound to be. But after that, who knew? I had been expensively schooled, but had not learnt shorthand or typing. I was not domesticated; I was not artistic. I can't say, however, that I worried much about the future, except in those bleak moments when it seemed to me that the terrible tentacles of our educational system might fold themselves around me so inescapably that from childhood to the grave I should never be out of the schoolroom.

Bernard finished his tea, mopped his nose on another paper handkerchief, said that he'd be getting back to work now, and disappeared into his little cubbyhole of a study. For a time after that there was silence in it; then his typewriter started. It was noisy, but I did not mind it nearly as much as the tape recording of that awful woman's voice. The clatter did not stop my reading, and while I was reading I could peacefully unwind my dreadful piece of knitting and forget that I had ever attempted it.

I went on reading until about half past six, when I thought that it was time to start cooking; but when I put my book down, Janet said that she would do the cooking that evening, and asked me only to get out the sherry and take a glass to Bernard.

When I took it in to him, he was sitting staring straight ahead at a wall lined with reference books, while his hands rested on either side of his typewriter.

"Thanks," he said absently as I put the glass of sherry down beside him. But as I turned to go, he went on, "You know, Elspeth, like it or not, I've got to put over the idea that Teresa Swale never killed that child, because I'm speaking in her voice and that was all she kept saying—innocent, I'm innocent, I'm innocent and ill-used, driven from pillar to post, dragged down into the mud, and so on and so on, and always innocent. And I'm beginning to worry now that I haven't got it quite right and that the stuff isn't going to read as if she believed it herself."

"Why can't you have it published under your own name for a change, instead of pretending that she wrote it herself?" I asked. "Then that wouldn't matter, would it?"

"Oh, my child, did you never hear of the law of libel?" he asked. "This thing can only be published at all *because* she's written it herself, because she wants to have her say, and so on. Besides, odd though it may seem, I get paid a lot more for writing as Teresa Swale than I'd get if I produced almost the same thing under my own name."

"Even though you have to go half-and-half with her?"

"Even so. People get a kick out of pretending to themselves that they're reading the actual words of a possible murderess, which they naturally wouldn't get out of reading the undistinguished prose of Bernard Lincoln."

There was a bitterness in his voice which was not usually there. Generally he could make a joke of his ghosting activities and, as he had told Janet and me earlier, could genuinely find fascination in putting himself into the skins of the people whom he interviewed, taking down their incoherent, often unpleasant stories on his tape recorder, and then settling down in this tiny room to play the reels over and over to himself, taking notes and gradually reducing the rambling chaos to an orderly, readable, salable narrative.

I thought that Teresa Swale must have been undermining his morale as badly as she had mine.

"So, after all, you've decided she was a murderess," I said. "You think she did throw that poor child out of the window?"

He looked up at me with a sardonic grin. I remember noticing that his blue eyes seemed unusually big and bright.

"Look, she was acquitted," he said. "Let's leave it at that. One likes to sleep at night, doesn't one?"

"You haven't been doing an awful lot of sleeping the last few nights," I said.

"Oh, that's just work; that doesn't count," he said.

"Well, cheer up—Janet's doing the cooking, so for once you'll get something better than tinned tongue and damp lettuce."

I turned to go, but he thrust out one of his long arms and caught me by the hand.

"Elspeth, you're being awfully good to us both—do you know that, and have we thanked you as we ought to?"

I was startled and embarrassed, made one of the silly sort of answers that one makes to members of one's own family circle who suddenly become emotional, and went out rather hurriedly. After a moment I heard his typewriter start again.

Pouring out a glass of sherry for myself, I went out to the kitchen with it.

"You know, I think you're right; Bernard's probably got a bit of a temperature," I said. "He's flushed and his eyes are sort of brilliant. I suppose it's flu."

"Thank heaven he's got the job practically finished then," Janet said. "There isn't a chance he'll stay in bed till it is. But if he clears the whole thing up this evening, he can be ill in peace tomorrow."

She was whisking eggs for a cheese soufflé and was enjoying herself. After the first three months, during most of which she'd been kept in bed by the doctor, she could actually have done far more of the work in the flat than she did, and she would have liked to do it. It was Bernard, making her carry the load of his anxiety as well as her own, who liked to see her taking life very quietly.

"A thousand pounds," she went on, "will be a wonderful tonic for him."

"A thousand pounds for him and a thousand pounds for Teresa—*Alarum* pay well, don't they?" I said.

"Look at their circulation," Janet said. "They can afford to. Have you laid the table, Elspeth?"

I had propped myself against the doorpost and was sipping my sherry. I was thinking about the child who had fallen out of a window in a house in Gloucestershire, a child three years old, whose picture in the newspapers of five years ago I vaguely remembered. A round-faced, round-eyed little boy with a sweet, smiling mouth and fat little hands clasping a toy dog.

To kill such a child would be about as hideous an action as human nature could achieve. Evil for evil's sake, motiveless, profitless.

Yet perhaps, I thought, Teresa Swale really was innocent. The jury, who had also had to listen to the soft, petulant whine of her voice, had thought so. So who was I to start working up this fury of prejudice against her? As Janet repeated her request to me to lay the table, I decided to stop thinking about the whole matter, thankful that I should never have to come face to face with Teresa Swale myself and have the responsibility, with her questioning eyes on mine, of making up my mind about her.

Supper was a silent meal, because Bernard, although he was sitting at the table, really was not with us. Afterwards, as soon as Janet had poured out the coffee, he picked up his cup and took it away to his room, and almost immediately the typewriter started again.

"I do hope he isn't going to keep you awake half the night," Janet said uneasily, hoping that I would say that just for once it wouldn't matter.

Knowing that what I said on this particular evening would not make much difference anyway, I obliged her by saying it, then started the washing up.

As it happens, I usually find the rattle of a typewriter quite soothing, and that night the tapping of the keys, coming as it did in uneven waves of sound, changed in my dreams into the soft pounding of waves on the shingle of a cool, lonely beach. Because of coming to look after Janet, I had had no summer holiday so far, and to go wandering along the edge of that dream sea, with the cool water lapping about my ankles, was very pleasant.

But presently, as a dream so often does, it turned frightening, though I do not remember what happened, apart from the fact that the beach changed into a railway station and that there were a great many people about and trains going in and out very noisily. Then everything was suddenly silent and I found that I was awake, with Bernard tiptoeing quietly through the room to the door.

He saw that I was awake and lifted a hand in a gesture of triumph to tell me that the job was finished, then crept out.

Next morning his cold was worse and it was obvious, just by looking at him, that he had a temperature, but he would not let Janet keep him in bed. He said he intended to get his manuscript off to *Alarum* that day if it was the last thing he did, and soon after breakfast he set off with it. The features editor, Tom Sammons, was a friend of his, and Bernard arranged by telephone, just before starting out, to have lunch with him.

Yet at half past eleven Bernard came home by taxi.

Janet was out in the garden at the back of the house and did not see the taxi or hear Bernard coming down the steps into the area. That was lucky, for he was walking as if he did not feel sure that his feet belonged to him, and when I ran to the door to meet him, he peered at me strangely, as if he did not know who I was. But when I asked him what was wrong, he said, "Nothing—nothing at all."

"The story——?"

For a moment I thought that the life story of Teresa Swale, on which he had worked so hard and for which he and Janet so badly needed the money, must have been thrown back at him. Yet I knew that the story had been commissioned and that *Alarum*, whatever might be said of it as a paper, had always treated him well.

And, as it turned out, that was not the trouble.

"Fine," Bernard answered. "Fine. Tom's going to give me a ring to say what he thinks of it sometime later today or tomorrow. Oh, the story's all right. I'll just have to show that woman a carbon of the thing and get her signature to the statement that she agrees to its being published under her name, and that'll be that. I meant to go on and do that this afternoon, but I don't think I will. I'll leave it till tomorrow."

He was talking fast and jerkily, as if he felt that he had to hurry to get the words out. Walking past me across the little hall, he went straight into the bedroom and sat down on the edge of the bed.

Taking his head in his hands, he said, "I'm just not feeling too good. It's nothing to worry about. Don't say anything to worry Janet. But I think I'll go to bed after all. I'll take a couple of aspirins and get into bed and go after that signature tomorrow."

He started to tug at his tie as if it were strangling him.

Of course I had to tell Janet, and once she had taken a look at him, there was no way to stop her worrying, because Bernard's temperature was a hundred and one. She called the doctor. It was about two hours before he arrived, and by then Bernard's temperature was already higher. The doctor did not say much, but without its having been asked of him, he told us that he would call in again later in the day.

By the time that the doctor arrived, Bernard had begun to talk in a rambling way and could not be kept quiet. His temperature was a hundred and four, and it was pneumonia.

CHAPTER TWO

At that stage the doctor was really more anxious about Janet than about Bernard. But as soon as Bernard became ill, Janet forgot to worry about herself and, transferring all her fears to him, turned into something like her normally brisk self. Bernard's ramblings, which went on intermittently throughout the evening and through most of the night, filled her with a peculiarly intense terror and, to keep her mind off them, she started doing all sorts of little jobs about the house. When there was no cooking to be done, or hot drinks to be made, she invented other jobs.

Bernard's mutterings were mostly connected with Teresa Swale, and gruesome some of them sounded. The little boy who had fallen out of a window five years before was all confused in his mind with Janet's child. I remember that Tom Sammons rang up sometime in the evening and said that the story was a grand piece of work, and I told this to Bernard, thinking that it might ease his mind. He managed to take it in, smiled brilliantly, and said that all that was needed now was Teresa's signature and that he'd get it tomorrow. But presently it appeared that it had been a mistake to give him Tom's message,

12

for now Bernard talked more and more about the importance of getting the signature quickly, so that *Alarum* would pay him, and, suddenly deciding that it was morning, he said that he must get up and go to see her. Janet quietened him down, and towards morning he fell into a deep sleep.

But he did not react to the penicillin that he had had in the way that he should have. When the doctor came again early next day I guessed from his peculiarly calm expression and level voice that things were not going as he had expected.

If Janet thought this, too, she said nothing about it. Altogether she said very little. Soon after breakfast she asked me to do a little shopping for her, gave me a list, and hurried me off. Since none of the things on the list was urgent, I thought that she must simply want me out of the way for a little while. As soon as I returned, she told me her reason. Beckoning me into the sitting room, she sat down at the table and pointed at the chair opposite—which was a way she had when she thought that we ought to have a serious discussion—and said, "Elspeth, I wanted to be alone so that I could think something out. The fact is, I think one of us ought to go and get that signature from Teresa Swale. I think it would help."

"It probably would," I agreed.

"I don't mind which of us goes," she went on. She was looking white and exhausted, but her manner was determined. "If you don't like the idea of it, I'll go and you can stay here with Bernard. But the sooner it's done, I think, the better."

"I'll go," I said.

"Are you sure?" she said. "From what Bernard told me, it's a pretty frightful place she lives in, and she's a fairly horrible sort of woman. I don't like asking you to go."

"Of course I'll go," I said. "Straight away. You get what rest you can."

"You've only got to give her the carbon of the story and get her to sign a statement that it can be printed under her name. I've got that typed out in the form Bernard generally uses. You probably won't even have to go inside the house. All the same . . ."

13

She was worrying because Teresa Swale's slide downwards in the world after her acquittal, which had been the substance of the story that she had told to Bernard, had carried her from the honourable occupation of children's nurse into prostitution, and it seemed to Janet that to ask her baby sister to interview her was a shocking demand to make, even though the baby sister had a degree in history, which is a subject which does not leave one as innocent as it might.

"Look," I said, "if Bernard even started to imagine you'd gone out to get that signature, his temperature would jump right over the roof. And you're the one who's really needed here."

"Bless you," she said and held out a hand to me.

I told her again to try to get some rest, took the papers she gave me, put a comb through my hair—which is fair and springy like hers, but cut shorter—put some fresh lipstick on, and, as I went to the door, told her that unless Teresa Swale was out, in which case I would wait for her, I should be back in a couple of hours at the most.

"No," Janet said quickly, "don't wait. If she isn't in, just come straight back. We can always tell Bernard you've got the signature, even if you haven't. Then you can try again later."

"All right," I promised, and she gave me an uncertain smile as I went out.

It was about ten o'clock then, which seemed strange, because, as I had been up most of the night, it felt far later. But the air still had a morning freshness. There had been rain in the night, and the leaves of the plane trees had a temporary cleanness. The sky was clear and later on, I thought, it would probably be hot.

I made for Adelaide Road, where I could get a bus straight to Tottenham Court Road. Almost immediately one came; it was almost empty, because it was late for people going to work, but early for the shopping crowds. Going to the front of the bus, I slumped into a seat and, as I did so, realised how much the night had taken out of me and how tired I was. Working at the job of keeping awake, I started thinking about the story of Teresa Swale.

I did not really know much about it. I have always been lazy about reading newspapers, and when I have taken a look at the headlines,

14

to make sure that no one is going to war with anyone that day, I usually look only at the book reviews and cinema notices, and then use the paper for wrapping up the potato peelings and fishbones before putting them into the dustbin.

And five years ago I had been even less interested in public affairs than I am now, unless they were the public affairs of about three hundred years ago. That was a period that had a great fascination for me, and I would sit at breakfast reading about Prince Rupert and Montrose, instead of about what was happening in the world around me.

What I knew about the Swale case was mostly what Bernard had told me at odd moments during the last few days. I knew that Teresa Swale was the daughter of a small builder in the Midlands. The family was respectable, not badly off, and Teresa had been given a good education. When she had decided to become a children's nurse, she had been properly trained, then had had one or two jobs before going to work for Mrs. Hill in Gloucestershire.

At that time Teresa was twenty-two, was charming and conscientious, and pleased everybody. Bernard had a photograph of her as she had been then. Her face was oval and long with large, mild eyes, with very long lashes, and a small mouth which was closed in a gentle pout. It did not look a vicious face, though there was something about it that I did not like, a sort of emptiness, a lack of something. Her hair was dark and parted in the middle. Her neck was long and slender. There was a touch of the wilting flower about her, a drooping sort of sweetness.

Mrs. Hill was a young widow with one son, David, aged three. Mrs. Hill had met and married her husband in the Sudan. He had been a colonel and was a good deal older than she and came of a wealthy family. When he was killed in a motor accident, his wife had come to England and settled into the house in the village of Footfield, which had belonged to the Hills for several generations. Teresa Swale had been engaged as a nurse for David almost immediately. David was said to have liked her, and she had shown every sign of liking the child, and everything had seemed to be going smoothly until, about a month after Teresa's arrival, David had been found dead on a paved path in front of the house, having fallen out of an upper-storey window.

Murder was suspected almost at once, because the window—out of which it could be shown that David had fallen, since there had been some threads from his jersey caught on a splinter on the sill—was too high for him to have been able to climb up to it by himself, unless there had been a chair or other piece of furniture under it; and it happened that the window was in a passage and that there had been no furniture of any kind near it.

The information that led to the arrest of Teresa Swale came later in the day from a passing motorist. He had gone to the police with his story as soon as he heard on the radio of the death of the child. The man had told them that he had driven past the house at just the time when David was thought to have fallen and had seen at the window a dark-haired girl in a green dress, holding a struggling child. Further, he had said that it had been his impression that the girl had actually been thrusting the child out of the window, rather than pulling him back. Asked why, in that case, he had not stopped and protested, he had answered that he had passed the house before he had really taken in what he had seen, but that he had then backed his car until he was again opposite the window and that by then there had been no sign of the girl or the child. Supposing that all was well, therefore, he had driven on.

In fact, it was then supposed, the body of the child, lying on the path, had been hidden from the road by a hedge, where the motorist could not see it.

Teresa Swale had not denied having been at the window with David in her arms. She had not even denied holding him out of the window. But she had said that she had found him standing on a chair under the window and trying to climb onto the sill, and that she had snatched him up, scolded him, held him out of the window to show him just how far he could have fallen, and then sent him along to his nursery and removed the chair.

Asked how she thought that the chair had come to be under the

window, she had replied that she supposed David himself had dragged
it there. She had said that it was a light wooden chair which came
from Mrs. Hill's bedroom, the door of which was almost opposite
the window. Teresa had also said that she had had trouble before with
David about climbing onto that window sill. He had seen the pink
flowers of a clematis hanging round it and wanted to pick them. On
this occasion she had decided to give him a lesson.

The housekeeper, however, who had been with the Hills for years,
had denied that David had had any habit of climbing onto that
window sill, and had added that more than once she had protested
on hearing Teresa threatening the child with being thrown out of
the window if he would not keep quiet. Some flakes of paint from
the outer edge of the window frame were found on the sleeve of
Teresa's green dress, and she was arrested for murder.

Her trial was a very short one. It had turned out that there
were traces of mud from David's shoes on the seat of the chair by
his mother's bed and also the prints of sticky little hands on the legs
and the back of the chair. Also it had emerged that the clock by which
the motorist had gauged the time at which he had passed the house
and seen the incident of the girl at the window had been the clock
in his car, and that it was exceedingly unreliable, tending to run so
fast that it was almost certain that the incident had taken place at
least a quarter of an hour earlier than he had first stated. A few minutes after the time when the motorist had really passed the house,
the gardener, knocking off work to go home to lunch, had passed along
the path under the window, and there had been no body on it. After
deliberating for less than an hour, the jury had brought in a verdict
of not guilty, and Teresa had left the court without, it had been made
very clear by the judge, a stain on her character.

Yet she had never been able to get another job as a children's
nurse.

She had had other jobs. She had been a waitress, a chambermaid
in a hotel, a charwoman in various offices. But sooner or later, so she
had told Bernard in the thin, complaining voice that had got so badly
on my nerves, the story of the death of little David Hill had always

caught up with her. She had always found herself ostracized, and sooner or later dismissed. In the end she had drifted on to the streets.

She was living now in one of the small, squalid streets between Russell Square and the Grays Inn Road. When I found it, I did not think that it looked particularly squalid, for the houses were handsome, with well-proportioned windows and delicate fanlights. The first breath of squalor came only after I had rung one of the odd collection of bells beside one of those dignified doorways and the door had been opened.

Literally I breathed the squalor in then—a smell of aged dirt and neglected drains, of stale food and stale human bodies. An old woman stood in the doorway, looking at me with her wide, hairy nostrils quivering, as if she, in her turn, were sniffing suspiciously at the strangeness of my smell.

She was probably tall, but she stooped so far forward that she seemed to be several inches shorter than I was, and she had to twist her big head sideways to look up at me. The loose, print overall that she wore hung straight from her neck to the ground, hiding all the queer, misshapen bulk behind it. Behind her I saw uncarpeted stairs and peeling wallpaper.

Her voice was a loud, ingratiating rasp. "Well, my duck?"

"Does Miss Swale live here?" I asked.

"Ain't in," she answered.

"Do you know when she'll be back?" I asked.

"How'd I know that?" she said.

"Well, it's rather important," I said. "I just hoped you might know."

"Well, I generally knows," she said. "That's right, I does."

"If you'd just tell me when you expect her, I'll come back," I said.

"Well, I don't really expect her, my duck," she said. "That's why I can't tell you when she'll be back."

"Do you mean she's moved away?" I asked. "Gone to another address?"

"Why'd she do that?" she asked. "She's all right here."

"Anyway, she's out—you're sure she's out?"

"She's out, that's right," she said.

"You're quite sure? You don't think it might be worth looking in her room? It really is important. It's—it's about some money that's coming to her."

The old woman's watery eyes focussed on me sharply for a moment, then she gave a shake of her head. "Look, I been in and out of her room half a dozen times—I know she ain't there," she said.

"How long ago did she go out?"

"Two-three days."

I was aghast. "Days!"

"That's right," she said.

"And she didn't say anything to you about how long she meant to be away?"

"Why'd she do that?" she asked.

"Aren't you her landlady?"

"That's right. She rents my back room."

"I think I'd better call back later," I said. "Meanwhile, if she comes in, would you be so kind as to give her this?"

I took a notebook out of my handbag, tore out a page, wrote the Lincolns' telephone number on it, and held it out.

"And I'd be very grateful," I said, "if you'd tell her it's really important. It's about the thousand pounds that's coming to her."

"A thousand pounds—well!" the old woman said.

I saw that I had made a mistake. She could not believe in any thousand pounds. The old eyes became sharp again, but with the glitter of mockery.

"So Teresa's come into a thousand pounds—and run out on it! That's good, eh? And just where do you come into it, my duck?"

It seemed to me that to explain would have taken much too long.

"I'm a lawyer's clerk," I said briskly, "and I've got a paper for her to sign so that she can get the money."

She folded the page from my notebook up small and thrust it down deep into one of the bulging pockets of her overall. I doubted if it would ever see the light of day again.

"Teresa's come into a thousand pounds and you're a lawyer's clerk and you got a paper for her to sign," she said, as if she were repeating a lesson; but, as she turned away, closing the door in my face, I heard her chuckling hoarsely.

I walked slowly away. As I had expected, the day was growing warmer. The coat I was wearing over a cotton dress began to feel too heavy, and one of the moods came on, which do not afflict me often, of feeling stifled by the buildings and the people around me and of longing to be almost anywhere but in London. I love London, and I had made no plans for my future, apart from my stint at that school in Nottingham, which did not mean living in London. But I had grown up in Berkshire, in a village close to the downs, and on certain days the noise and the smell of streets, the constant pressure of people, and the impossibility of looking through the blackened walls of the buildings to any distant horizon settled on my spirits like a smothering physical load. To make things worse, the people I passed all started to turn into Teresa Swale and had probably, at some time in their pasts, thrown children out of windows. Theobald's Road became a graveyard.

I was suffering, I suppose, from having lived for the last few weeks at such close quarters with Janet and Bernard. I had always been fond of them both and considered that I was unusually lucky in my family. This was fortunate, because by then they were all the family I had. All the same, older sisters allow themselves to voice criticisms of one's personal habits, which no one else would venture to express, and at the same time tend to regard it as a criticism of themselves if one chooses a path in life completely different from the one that they have trodden. In any normal couple of months together Janet and I would have had three or four very outspoken discussions of our two characters, our voices growing louder as the arguments proceeded, and eventually one or two very nasty and unforgivable things would be said, for which deep apologies would be offered an hour or two later.

But this time there had been no such outlet. Every time that our voices had started to rise, I had seen Bernard looking across the room at me with such an imploring look in his squinting eyes that I had gulped down the next sentence and forced myself to agree with Janet that I was terribly ignorant and juvenile for my age, was lazy and untidy, did not take enough care of my hair and my nails, did not take enough exercise, read a lot of rubbish, and made friends only with deplorably feckless and untrustworthy people.

The odd thing was that on all these points I was almost entirely in agreement with Janet, but that made me only resent what she said the more. One should not, I thought, forgetting all the pointed things I had said to her from time to time, be eternally rubbing other people's noses in their own shortcomings, because, after all, it's they, poor things, who have to live with them. On the way back to Hampstead I worked myself up into a querulous state of feeling much abused and undervalued.

I forgot all about it the moment I turned into the road where Bernard and Janet lived and saw the ambulance in front of the house.

Since getting off the bus, I had been walking along with dragging feet, my coat hanging open because of the growing heat of the day, my shoulders drooping. But as soon as I saw the ambulance, the St. John's men in their dark blue uniforms, and Janet standing forlornly at the gate with two or three neighbours gathered round her, I started to run. But before I reached the gate, the ambulance had driven off.

Janet and I did not say anything to each other. She thanked the neighbours quietly for their kind inquiries and we went down the area steps together. The flat seemed dark and airless. We went into the sitting room, Janet dropped into her usual chair and looked round her with a vague, lost stare, and then her eyes settled on my face and I flinched at the pain in them.

"It's all right; there isn't anything to worry about," she said tonelessly. "It's just that for some reason the penicillin doesn't seem to have done its stuff and Dr. Gray thinks he'll be better off in hospital, where they can try some of the other things and keep an eye on him all the time."

"It'll be better for you, at any rate," I said. "I expect that's the real reason they've moved him."

"Yes," she agreed, "I expect that's it. I really don't think there's anything to worry about. I mean, pneumonia isn't really serious, is it? Not nowadays."

"Of course not," I said.

"They'll give him some of those other drugs, and they're certain to work."

"Oh yes."

"They're taking him to St. Bride's and I can go and see him later today."

"Then you'd better have a rest now," I said, and started plumping up the cushions on the divan. "Come and lie down and I'll get us some lunch."

She did not stir, except to lean her head back in the chair. I saw the beads of moisture on her forehead and I noticed how her hands gripped the arms of the chair.

I stood looking helplessly at her, thinking that there must be something that I could do for her, but not even able to think of anything more to say.

After a moment, in the same expressionless voice, she said, "That woman—did you see her and get her to sign that paper?"

"She was out," I said. "I'll try again this afternoon."

"Out?" Janet said sharply. All the terror in her heart had put a fine edge on her perceptions and she had heard something in my voice which I had not intended should be there. "You mean you couldn't find her; you don't know where she is?"

"I just mean she was out," I said. "I saw her landlady and I left this telephone number with her and also I said I'd be back presently."

Janet drew an unsteady breath. "We need that signature, Elspeth —we need it terribly badly, now that Bernard's so ill. It's partly to stop him worrying about it, but we're quite a bit overdrawn, too, and now that there won't be anything else coming in for some time. . . ." She stopped, and her features twitched in a curious nervous grimace as she resisted the onset of tears. "Well, it's no good worrying, is it?" she said.

I went over to her and put my hands on her shoulders.

"It really isn't," I said, "when all I've got to do is go back after we've had some lunch and find her. And I promise you I'll do that—I'll find Teresa and get that signature out of her straight away, if it kills me."

CHAPTER THREE

I made some coffee and some sandwiches and afterwards, while Janet rested, I changed out of my crumpled cotton dress into a blue linen suit and set out again on the hunt for Teresa Swale. But I was not expecting to find her. I knew that this was one of those days on which everything was going to go wrong.

What I was to do if I did not find her, I had no idea. But a promise is a promise. I was thinking about this awkward fact and turning one or two plans over in my mind and not really noticing that I was almost at Teresa's door when I realised that it had just opened and closed and that a man had come out and was walking towards me.

He was short, slender, well-dressed, and in a hurry. As he went rapidly past me, I noticed that he was deeply tanned, as if he had just come back from abroad, and that he was frowning a frown of hard thought. He seemed wholly absorbed in whatever was on his mind and unaware of what was around him.

Yet as I stopped at the door from which he had just emerged, he stopped, too, about twenty yards up the pavement, and gave me a sharp stare. But as the door was opened by the old crone whom I had seen in the morning, he turned away and walked off.

The old woman gave a throaty chuckle which sent a hot breath of gin into my face and, before I could speak, she said, "No, my duck."

"Miss Swale hasn't come back?"

There was malicious pleasure at my disappointment in her watery eyes as she shook her big, frowzy head.

"No, but you can go on coming and asking, can't you? There's no one can stop you doing that," she said.

"I can think of more useful ways of spending my time," I said, "if she isn't likely to come."

"Ah well," she said with a sigh of mock gravity, "some people value their time."

I thought she made this sound like an eccentricity which she accepted tolerantly, though without understanding. But then my slow-moving mind got to work and I realised that there had been a slight emphasis on the word value.

Opening my handbag, I brought out a ten-shilling note. In deep embarrassment, I began, "If there's anything at all you could tell me to help me find her, I should be most awfully grateful . . ."

A dirty old hand reached out and I had just enough presence of mind to step back out of reach.

"Well now," she said, her eyes on the money, "let me think. It's a pity you should have to waste your time coming and going, ain't it? Yes, I know how it is; you'll be needed at the office. Well now, have you tried Callie?"

"Who's Callie?" I asked.

"Callie Mars. Friend of Teresa's. If anyone'd know, Callie would. She was here the day Teresa left—Callie and Lance were, both."

"Where does Callie live?"

The old woman gave me an address in one of the streets off Charlotte Street. Then, having parted with that piece of information as if it gave her a pain to do so, she suddenly seemed anxious to tell me more.

"Maybe you'll find Teresa with Callie; they're great friends, those two girls," she said. "Though why'd Teresa take her zip bag to go and stay with Callie, that's what I been asking myself. She's took the bag and her grey suit and the fruit salts, like she was meaning to stay away. But she's left the black skirt and the nylon blouse she bought a week back and the lovely pearl earrings she liked. They're there, right in the chest of drawers where I could help myself to them, only that I'm honest. So the way I think is, she's gone off for a day or two and she'll be coming back and maybe she's with Callie, or maybe Callie can tell you where she's gone. She's a nice girl, Callie, but you want to watch out for that Lance, if he's there." Her hand crept out again invitingly. "And that's a lot more information than I told the gentleman, even though he did leave his name and address, because the way I look at it is, it's queer him wanting her like that and leaving his name and address, and I wouldn't want to get Teresa into trouble. Now with you it's different, because you're a nice girl and you come from a lawyer's about some money for Teresa and you told me about it all fair and aboveboard. But the gentleman didn't say anything except to leave his name and address. And there's something about that makes me wonder. Doesn't it make you wonder, my duck?"

I agreed that it did.

"All the same, you took him into Miss Swale's room, didn't you?" I said.

"You want to see her room?" Her eyes held mine with the fierce concentration of greed. "I'm not sure I ought to allow that, even for you, my dear. After all, she trusts me, Teresa does."

In the end I parted with a pound for a glimpse of Teresa's room and also the name and address of the man whom I had seen come out of the house just as I arrived.

I wanted to see the room only to make sure that Teresa really was away, but what I saw did not tell me much, one way or the other. It was a small room on the ground floor, unexpectedly clean and tidy, but otherwise characterless. The black skirt and nylon blouse of which the landlady had spoken were on a hanger that hung from a peg on the back of the door. There were two pairs of high-heeled shoes under the bed. Some dog's-eared magazines were neatly stacked on the chest of drawers.

The old woman insisted on opening several of the drawers to show me that Teresa had left underclothes and stockings behind; and in one drawer, which otherwise was almost empty, she showed me a battered cardboard box, in which there were a few oddments of costume jewellery, including a pair of imitation pearl earrings, the size of halfpennies.

As she showed me these, the old woman gave a chuckle, took them out of the box, clipped them onto her own ears, and preened in front of the looking glass.

"See?" the old woman said. "Lovely, aren't they? She only got herself these last week and she liked herself in them all right. And the blouse, too. So she'll be coming back." She pointed at an old trunk in the corner of the room. "Besides, she left her luggage. She just took the zip bag and that wouldn't hardly take more than her night things. So she'll be back any time now, you can count on that. That's what I said to the gentleman, too."

I was looking curiously at the trunk. It had initials on it, but they were not Teresa's. They were R.O.H. I wondered if it was possible that the H stood for Hill.

"Oh yes, the gentleman," I said. "You were going to tell me his name and address."

She fished in the deep pocket of her overall, brought out a card, and let me look at it. The name written on it gave me a shock. It was Roy Carney, that incredibly prolific writer of paperback thrillers, Westerns, science fiction, and sword-and-cloak stuff, which for the last two or three years had been covering almost every bookstall in the country.

At first the shock was only one of surprise at seeing a well-known name. But as I left the house and walked towards the bus stop in Theobald's Road, meaning next to visit Callie Mars, the surprise turned into something more unpleasant. It became an unnerving suspicion that if Roy Carney was after Teresa, and so openly that he had no qualms about leaving his name and address with her landlady, it could only mean that he had decided that he wanted to use her life story. And if so, he might easily be ready to pay even more for it than *Alarum*, and in that case, what would become of all Bernard's hard work and his hopes?

It seemed to me that there was no time to be lost in finding Teresa.

The street in which Callie Mars lived was narrow and noisy with traffic. Cars and vans stood nose to tail alongside the one pavement. When some driver attempted to extricate his own vehicle, it provoked a great deal of shouting and unhelpful advice from exasperated taxi drivers, caught by the blockage, and drab characters lounging in doorways. Callie's room was over a small tailor's shop. Most of the name over his window had faded into smeary illegibility, but what was left of it looked Polish. The window was grimy and the bolt of cloth in it, draped over a chair, looked as if it had hung there in the same folds for years. A handwritten notice on a piece of paper, yellow with age and stuck to the glass with strips of stamp-paper, said, "Alterations."

The only door to the house seemed to belong to the tailor, but when I opened it, I found a short, dark passage and a staircase ahead of me. The entrance to the shop itself was a door on the right. Passing it, I started up stairs covered in linoleum treacherously frayed at the edge of each step. A yellow-eyed cat sat watching me come from a half landing, but as soon as I came near, it shot down to the street, a black streak of fear and hatred, spitting as it passed me.

On the floor above I found a door with a strip of cardboard pinned on to it, with the word Mars written on it in block letters. There was no bell or knocker, so I rapped with my knuckles. After a moment the door was thrown open and a young woman, looking as if she had had a string of words ready to snap out in my face, slowly closed her mouth and stood looking at me in surprise.

She was tall and angularly, gauntly handsome. Her hair was red, slightly curly and cut about the same length all over her head, and sticking out from forehead, temples, and the nape of her neck like the threads of a polishing mop. She had thin, delicate features and dark eyes so big and so blank and with such dark circles round them that they seemed merely to be openings into the shadowy places of her brain. She wore tight, tapered slacks of black velvet; a pale yellow sleeveless blouse that showed the sharp bones of her shoulders and elbows; and round her neck a string of enormous glass beads.

At first her strange eyes showed only surprise because I was not the person whom she had expected. Then the way that the lids narrowed around them gave them an expression of suspicion and hostility. There was a grim sort of amusement in the way she asked, "Well, what do *you* want?"

Her voice startled me because, although it was a hard, rough voice, it was educated.

"I'm very sorry to disturb you, but I'm looking for Miss Swale," I said. "I was told you might be able to tell me where she'd gone."

"Who told you that?" she asked.

"Her landlady."

"What d'you want Teresa for?"

With the possibility that Roy Carney was also on Teresa's trail, I had no intention of telling the truth about why I wanted her, so I stuck to the story that I had told the old woman.

"I'm a lawyer's clerk and I've got some papers for her to sign," I said. "It's to do with some money she's come into."

"God Almighty, then she was telling the truth!" Callie Mars said. "I don't know where she is, but come inside. I'll tell you anything I can."

She stood aside and gestured with one thumb for me to enter.

The room was in confusion. I imagine it always was, because it was a part of the confusion of mind of the woman who lived in it. Most of the furniture was of the cheapest, and I suppose it had been rented with the room, but besides the iron bedstead, the chipped, painted chest of drawers, and a table, the varnished top of which had been scarred by bottles and hot saucepans, there were some charming water-colours on the flyblown walls, a beautiful little walnut bureau, and one old and faded but lovely rug on the floor. All over the room there was a litter of clothes, tins of food, cosmetics, and unwashed crockery;

but also, under the window, there was a collection of flowering plants in pots—geraniums, begonias, water balsams, fuchsias—which had the air of having been carefully and skilfully tended.

Callie Mars removed a pair of shoes from a chair and said, "Sit down."

She sat down herself on the edge of the bed, took a cigarette out of a packet, and pushed the packet across the table towards me.

"Well, go on," she said. "Teresa's come into money from her husband and you want her to sign something, but she's vanished. That sounds queer to me. It doesn't really sound awfully like Teresa. If it was she who owed someone some money, that'd be different. I lent her some money once and I kissed good-bye to it long ago."

I stared at her. "Did you say her husband?"

Bernard had never mentioned a husband.

"Isn't that who it is?" she said. "That's what she told me. No, she didn't—she said she was going to get some money out of her husband's family. I didn't pay much attention, because she's always been full of schemes for laying her hands on some money. And I wasn't even inclined to take the husband quite seriously. And now here you are with papers to sign and all, which just goes to show—something or other."

She crossed one thin leg over the other and clasped her bare ankle in her hands. As her dull, cavernous eyes explored my face, I felt as if I were being looked at by some small, secret animal that lived permanently hidden away inside her skull.

"But you needn't worry," she went on. "If there's money in it, she'll be back."

"I'd hoped very much you'd be able to tell me where to find her," I said. "These things take such a long time to go through in any case that it's a pity to have any unnecessary delays."

She shook her head. "I'm sorry. I'd help if I could, but I haven't seen her since the day before yesterday, when she told me this thing about getting some money from her husband's family. I remember I said 'What husband?' and she said 'You'd be surprised if I told you.' And that isn't my idea of a very convincing answer, and anyway I was busy with my plants. . . ."

She stood up suddenly, walked across the room to the window, and picked up a jampot in which a sliver of something green was sprouting.

"I don't know why it is I've had no luck at all this year with my cuttings from my balsam," she said fretfully. "Usually I do well with them; I've got a green thumb. Everything grows for me. But this year, I don't know. . . ."

She gave a frowning shake of her head. She was standing between me and the window and, as she bent over the row of plants, I seemed to see her for an instant not in her sleeveless yellow blouse and tight velvet slacks but in old tweeds and gardening gloves and standing in a greenhouse, while in her drawing room near at hand the rug on the floor here, the watercolours, and the bureau filled their rightful places.

Wondering very much what had happened to Callie Mars that that should be a delusion and not the true picture, I asked, "Are you a close friend of Miss Swale's?"

"What you and I call close friends might be different," she said. "Teresa and I know the worst about each other and we put up with each other. But we don't always know just what the other's up to—if that's what you're really trying to ask—and I don't suppose either of us trusts the other any farther than she can see her, if as far. Why?"

"I was just wondering if you happened to know if she's been in touch recently with Roy Carney," I said.

"Who's he?" she asked.

"Who's——"

If she really did not know, she had not got eyes in her head. For even if she had never read a single book by Roy Carney, even if she never read anything at all, she could hardly have helped seeing his name on the bookstalls. She would have had to walk through the world in a dream to have missed it.

But perhaps that was what she did, I thought, and then suddenly found myself wondering if it was out of drink or drugs that the dream bloomed.

"He's a writer," I said. "A very popular writer."

"Well, you wouldn't call Teresa literary," she said indifferently.

"It isn't important anyway." I was rather wishing I had not mentioned Roy Carney. I did not want Callie to be able to hand on the information to Teresa that he had been looking for her. "What's important is for me somehow to trace Miss Swale."

As I said this, I heard steps in the passage outside. The door opened and a man came in. He was sallow, somewhat bulky, and quiet-looking, the kind of man who would stand next to you in a bus queue, wearing a felt hat and mackintosh, without your really noticing his existence. He stood in the doorway now, looking first at me, then at Callie. As she met that look, Callie's manner, which had had a certain friendliness and frankness about it, seemed suddenly to become defensive and furtive. She held his gaze with uneasy intensity, conveying some message.

He came in and shut the door.

"Hullo, Lance, I was just about giving you up," Callie said, and her voice had altered, too. It had taken on a falsely bright tone and at the same time had become flatter in tone and more cockney. She turned to me. "This is Mr. Martin, who'll be just as interested as I am in what you've told me about Teresa."

"Teresa?" the man said, taking off his hat and showing his thick, fair hair, which was plastered to his scalp with so much hair oil that it shone with a greenish lustre. "Teresa, eh?"

"She's come into money—it's the truth she was telling us about that," Callie said, and gave a cackle of laughter.

It was so unlike the laugh that I should have expected from the woman who had been talking with me a moment before that I felt as if some other presence must have come into the room at the same time as the man.

Callie went on, "This young lady wants to find her to get her to sign some papers, but just when she's wanted, she's cleared off. Can you make any sense of that?"

The man shook his head, giving me what I thought was a rather stupid stare.

"Money, eh?" he said thoughtfully.

His face struck me as altogether a stupid one, plump and heavy, with small, blunt features of the kind which it would be very difficult to remember—pouchy eyelids over grey eyes and a plump, puckered

32

little mouth, which he seemed to prefer not to open if it could be avoided. Yet he made me feel uneasy and nervously anxious to get away.

"May I leave my telephone number with you?" I said to Callie Mars. "Then if Miss Swale comes back you could ask her to get in touch with me at once."

"All right," she answered. "What's the name I tell her? I don't think you ever told me your name."

"My name won't mean anything to her," I said. "Tell her to get in touch with Mr. Lincoln."

She hunted around in the litter on the table for a pencil with which to write down the telephone number.

The sight of her fumbling seemed to produce petulant irritation in Lance Martin. Putting a hand in his breast pocket, he brought out a pencil and threw it down on the table in front of her. The gesture had been so smooth and swift that for an instant I had felt a stab of preposterous fear that it was a knife that I was going to see in his hand. Even when I saw the pencil lying on the table, the fear did not quite die. When I had seen Callie write the number down, I stood up quickly and started towards the door.

I found that Lance Martin had somehow got in front of me.

"Who's this Lincoln?" he asked.

"He's—he's one of the partners in the firm," I answered. "But that's his private number. Miss Swale, of course, knows the number of the office."

Callie Mars moved forward so that she stood beside the man.

"And that Roy Carney—where does he come in?" she asked. "I don't think you finished telling me."

There was nothing threatening in the attitude of either of them, but there was no doubt about it—they were between me and the door.

"I wish I knew," I said. "Mr. Lincoln wishes he knew. But clients simply won't repose their confidence in their lawyers as fully as they ought. Lawyers and doctors—so often they aren't called in till it's too late. People are so afraid to talk frankly. . . ."

Chattering inanely, I took a step towards the door, wondering in a panicky way if there was actually any possibility, for reasons that I did not understand at all, that they would stop my leaving.

Lance Martin turned to the door himself and opened it for me and I felt extremely foolish.

"Well, thank you very much for being so helpful," I said, "and I'm sorry to have taken up so much of your time."

But as the door closed behind me, I went down the stairs almost as fast as the black cat that I had met on my way up.

Out in the street I felt ashamed of that mood of panic and wondered what on earth had brought it on. I had not felt at all nervous of Callie Mars as long as I was alone with her, and Lance Martin had done nothing but stand and look at me, produce a pencil when it was required, and open the door.

Drawing a deep breath, I looked up and down at the congealed traffic of the street, felt reassured, and decided that my sleepless night and my worry at being unable to find Teresa Swale had been the cause of the trouble and that what I needed was a cup of coffee. Walking on down the street, I went into a café and ordered coffee and one of the dry-looking buns on the counter.

Drinking the coffee and chewing my way through the bun, I tried to think of something more that I could do before going back to Hampstead and telling Janet how completely I had failed. Remembering what Callie Mars had told me of Teresa's expecting money from her husband's family, I wondered if there was any way that I could possibly discover who they were and where they lived. There was Somerset House, wasn't there? I could go there and ask for a copy of Teresa's marriage certificate. But it was too late for that today. The offices there would probably be closed already.

Besides, like Callie, I was not inclined to take the husband seriously. According to Bernard, Teresa had told her whole story, from infancy to the present day, with a shattering lack of inhibition, and I was sure that there had never been any mention of marriage. The likeliest explanation of the husband, I thought, was that she had invented him to account for the money that she was going to be paid by *Alarum*. Why she minded her friend's knowing about that I did not know, yet certainly there had been no hint from Callie Mars that she had any knowledge of Teresa's dealings with Bernard.

The likeliest explanation of her disappearance from her usual haunts at this awkward moment, I thought, was that she had gone away for a few days with some man, and in that case there was nothing to be done but wait until she came back again.

But if she had gone away with a man, why had she left behind the big pearl earrings she was so fond of and her new nylon blouse?

As I drank up the rest of the weak coffee, it seemed to me that there was only one thing that I could still do before returning to Janet and telling her that we should simply have to wait until Teresa took it into her head to return. I was not sure if it was a judicious thing to do, but at least if I did it, Janet could not say that I had not tried my hardest. So, first looking in my handbag to make sure that I had enough money, I paid my bill and went out, hailed a taxi, and told the driver to take me to the hotel where Roy Carney was staying.

In the taxi I relaxed in a corner with my eyes shut and tried to think out just what I was going to ask him when I saw him. I had still not quite made up my mind about this when I walked in at the unobtrusive doorway of the very expensive little hotel off Piccadilly and asked the reception clerk if I could see Mr. Carney.

She asked for my name and I answered, "I'm Miss Elspeth Purvis, but that won't mean anything to him. Please tell him it's in connection with Miss Swale."

She spoke into the house telephone and, after a moment, smiled and nodded.

"Mr. Carney will be down in a moment," she said. "Would you like to wait for him over there?" She pointed through an archway to a small lounge, which I was relieved to see was nearly empty.

I started towards it but, as I did so, a man's voice spoke behind me, and at what he said I stopped and turned quickly. For, like me, he was asking for Roy Carney, adding that Mr. Carney was expecting him and that his name was Hill.

CHAPTER FOUR

Like me, he was told that Mr. Carney would be down in a moment.

He followed me into the lounge, a place all in faint greens and greys, with fragile, gilded chairs. I sat down on one of these; then I decided I should feel better standing up; then I found that it was difficult not to start walking up and down, so I sat down again. I was more nervous than I had expected.

The man who had given the name of Hill, the same name as that of the child for whose murder Teresa Swale had been arrested, stood quietly near the entrance, and I had a good chance to look at him.

He was about six feet tall and fairly slender. His hair was dark and curly. His eyes were dark, with strongly marked, dark eyebrows ruled straight across his face and nearly meeting over a thin, bony nose. It was a thin face, almost haggard, hollow at the temples, with hollow cheeks under high cheekbones and a long pointed chin. He wore a tweed jacket and flannel trousers. His age, like Roy Carney's, was about thirty and, like Roy Carney when he had come away after

36

talking to Teresa's landlady, this man had something on his mind about which he was doing some very hard thinking.

We both heard the whine of the lift and the clang of its door opening. I stood up and went a few steps to meet the man who came out. The other man also went to meet him, but when he realised that we were both waiting for the same person, he gave me a disconcerted look and let me go ahead.

Roy Carney's glance settled on me for an instant, then went past me, and he made one of those small gestures of greeting which showed that he and the other man knew each other well. Then he looked back at me.

"You're Miss . . ." He hesitated, gave a smile, and said, "I'm sorry, I didn't really get your name."

"Purvis," I said.

"And you've got something to tell me about Teresa Swale?"

"No," I said, "it's something I want to ask you."

His eyebrows went up. They were thin and finely arched and much fairer than his deeply tanned skin. Like his hair, which would normally have been brown, they had the bleached look that can come from a strong dose of sunshine. Successful authors, I thought, were lucky people. They could live in the sun, if they wanted to. His face was a square, pleasant, healthy-looking face with undistinguished features. He was about the same height as I was, and his grey eyes, on a level with mine, looked straight into them with a shrewd, questioning stare.

"I've seen you before, haven't I?" he said.

"Yes," I said, "this afternoon."

He nodded. "I remember." He turned to the other man. "Hullo, Nick. Nice to see you. Miss Purvis, this is Nick Hill, a very old friend of mine. And it happens that he also wants to talk about Teresa Swale. So let's get down to it. But I think we might be better off in the bar, don't you?"

He cocked one of his mobile eyebrows at me again to see how I responded to the suggestion. I said I agreed, and we filed through the little lounge to a small, shadowy cocktail bar in which we were the first customers and where only the soundless movements of a white-coated bartender were to be seen in the murk.

The two men had let me go ahead of them and I knew that there had been some whispered exchange of a few words behind me. At the same time I had had a moment in which to think. I could not see myself, in this company, getting away with the story of being a lawyer's clerk, with papers in my handbag concerning a mysterious inheritance for Teresa to sign. But, since discovering that there was a connection between Roy Carney and the Hills, it no longer seemed to me that his reason for wanting to see Teresa had necessarily anything to do with a desire to use her life story. And if he was not in competition with Bernard, there was no reason why I should not tell him the truth about why I so badly needed to find her.

We sat down round a low table in one of the dark corners, and Roy Carney ordered the drinks. There were small dishes on the table filled with olives and potato crisps, and because of my nervousness I reached out at once for a potato crisp and, having had one, I could not stop myself having another. That is how they always affect me, and I remember crunching potato crisps all through the conversation that followed. When the dish was empty, Roy Carney signalled to the bartender to bring another, and the two men watched me eating as if I were a starving refugee just escaped over a dangerous frontier.

I found the beginning of the conversation extremely difficult, even though I had decided to tell the simple truth. Nicholas Hill had a paralyzing effect on me. Sitting silently, half turned away from me and not looking at me, he gave me the feeling that I had intruded into something in which I was very definitely not wanted. It was because of this feeling that I blurted out my first unconsidered question.

"Do you or don't you believe Teresa Swale was innocent?" I asked.

It was such a trite sort of beginning that as soon as it was out I was furious with myself, grabbed three potato crisps, and put them into my mouth quickly, one after the other.

The two men exchanged looks; then Roy Carney said, "You aren't a journalist, are you?"

"No," I said.

38

"This isn't an interview?"

"Oh no."

"Then why can it possibly matter to you what I think on that matter?"

"It doesn't really," I said, "except that it's got on to my own mind and it keeps popping out. What I really meant to ask you is whether the name Bernard Lincoln means anything to you?"

"Now he *is* a journalist," he said.

"Yes. And he's been doing a thing recently about Teresa Swale. He picked her up somehow in some Soho pub and they agreed he should ghost her life story for her. He does that quite often, mainly for *Alarum*, because they pay so awfully well. You know how it works—he gets her to talk on and on about herself onto a tape recorder; then he cuts it down to just a fraction of the whole amount and writes it up and then it gets published under her name, as if she'd actually written it herself."

"Yes, I've done some of that myself," Roy Carney said, "though I never managed to get into *Alarum*." He turned his head towards his friend. "Nick, what do you think about this?"

"I think it probably explains what's been puzzling you," Nicholas Hill answered. "A man like Lincoln knows a lot of what goes on behind the scenes, and he could have passed it on."

I did not understand this, but it was said with a sort of scorn in his voice which made me say hotly, "Bernard doesn't splash confidences about and he doesn't print anything like this without permission."

Roy Carney looked back at me and said peaceably, "No, of course not. Anyway, he's got his living to make. I could tell you some of the things I did before my yarns—God knows why—hit the market. I once ghosted a story for Leni Briefbach, the spy, before they executed her. D'you remember Leni? No, you'd be too young. The trouble was, being in Intelligence, it wasn't exactly correct on my part even to think of doing what I did; but there was something about Leni . . . it wasn't beauty exactly. She was really almost a plain woman. But there was a sort of intensity and power about her which made one feel that at a different moment in history, in a different environment, she might have become, say, a nun, or perhaps a doctor—at any rate, someone devoted to a very different ideal from the one that had taken her to that prison cell. . . ."

Nicholas Hill suddenly picked up his glass and set it down again on the table with a bang. It interrupted Roy Carney's reminiscence.

"Sorry," he said. "I wasn't trying to change the subject. Let's go back to Bernard Lincoln. He's been writing up Teresa's story, and you—that's still a puzzle. Where do you come in?"

"I'm his sister-in-law," I said, "and I've got to find Teresa for him, because she hasn't signed the paper that gives *Alarum* the right to publish his story under her name, and they won't pay him till they've got it."

"And why can't brother-in-law Bernard look for her himself?" he asked.

"Because he's in hospital with pneumonia," I answered.

I had not meant to put pathos into that. I had meant it to be a mere statement of fact. But tiredness, and a feeling that had been growing on me that coming here had been a bad mistake and that telling my story frankly with the Hill man there listening to it had been an even worse one, had produced such a state of tension in me that my voice shook on the words.

A change at once came over the two men. Nicholas Hill shot a quick, dismayed look at me, as if he expected me to burst into tears on the spot. Roy Carney showed a less self-conscious concern. He said, "That's rotten. I'm so sorry. But pneumonia's nothing to worry about nowadays, you know. They'll pump him full of penicillin and he'll be home again in no time. I had it myself a couple of years ago. The worst of it was I was in the middle of a book, or, rather, in the middle of about three books, dictating away to three different typists, and I started feeling worse and worse and I couldn't remember which one I was dictating to and all their faces started swimming into one. But I went on, because for the only time in my life I became absolutely certain I was inspired and that if I stopped, something simply terrific would be lost to mankind. It was only delirium, of course, and presently everything went black and I suppose, though I'm not quite sure, that I stopped dictating. Then I got better and realised that I'd better get hold of those manuscripts quickly and cut out the frantic nonsense I must have talked. But they'd all gone off to the publisher already with their stories all mixed up and the wrong endings on each of them. But d'you think I could get anyone to believe that? D'you think anyone ever noticed it? D'you think anyone but me knows it to this day? So don't worry about Bernard."

I laughed uncertainly. "Thank you," I said. "We aren't really worried. But it's rather important to find Teresa Swale, because fretting about it, as he's doing, can't be helping him, can it? And seeing you coming out of the house she lives in made me think that just possibly you might have some idea about where she'd gone."

"Just a minute," Roy Carney said. "How did you know who I was?"

"I got it out of her landlady."

"Did you indeed! Then you got more out of her than I did."

"Please, can't you suggest where she might have gone?" I said.

"I wish I could—I honestly do—but I can't. I want her myself for——" He gave a swift look at Nicholas Hill. "For a quite different sort of reason. But all I could get out of the old woman was that she went away a couple of days ago and didn't take all her belongings, so presumably she'll be back sometime, but just when is anybody's guess."

After a slight hesitation, because I could not quite decide whether what I was going to say next was a piece of cleverness or was utter stupidity, I said, "Teresa has a friend called Callie Mars. I got her name, too, out of the old woman, and I've just been to see her. She told me that all Teresa had told her was that she was going to collect some money that was coming to her from her husband's family. I thought—I wondered——" I looked from one to the other and found it extraordinarily difficult to go on because of the way that both their expressions altered. But then I managed to bring out the question that I had really come to ask. "I wondered, since you know her, if you've ever heard anything about a husband and could tell me where to find him."

Looking back, I realise clearly how that question must have sounded to them. Even a moment after I had asked it, with their faces telling me what they thought, it dawned on me that I could have seemed to be suggesting that the unknown husband of Teresa Swale might be Roy Carney himself, and that I now probably appeared to them a very sinister person.

Roy Carney looked at a loss. He gave me a helpless, bewildered stare and his tanned cheeks flushed slightly. I could feel my own cheeks flaming, but at least I had the sense not to rush on into explanations of what I had or had not meant, but to stay silent.

After a moment, Roy Carney's eyes moved uneasily away to meet his friend's, and I saw his pale eyebrows lift very faintly in a question. They seemed to understand each other, those two, remarkably well. Without any word being spoken between them, Nicholas Hill took charge of the interview.

Turning so that he faced me fully, looking me bleakly up and down, he said in a soft voice, "Miss Purvis, aren't you getting into rather deep water?"

His voice was a deep one, the kind that has resonance even when it is used hardly above a whisper.

I nodded my head, perhaps just a little too vigorously.

"I'm rather afraid of that, and as a matter of fact I don't much like it," I said, deciding that the easiest way out for me, unless he actually accused me of trying to blackmail Roy Carney, was to refuse to see what he was implying. "I've never had to do anything of this sort before. I went to see this Callie Mars and she turned out to be an extraordinary woman with a voice that sounded as if she'd come from Cheltenham Ladies' College, until her boy friend came into the room, and from then on you'd have thought she'd been born and bred in Soho. And she keeps rows and rows of potted plants in her room and says she's got green fingers. . . . But when her boy friend took a pencil out of his pocket, I thought from the way his hand moved that it was going to turn out to be a knife, and my heart nearly stopped. It was all nonsense and because I'm not accustomed to that sort of thing, but I don't think I've ever been so frightened . . ." I realised that I was overdoing the idiocy and stopped.

"You've an active imagination, haven't you?" Nicholas Hill said.

"So I've often been told," I answered.

"Like Roy," he said. "Roy's imagination is the envy of all who know him."

"No," I said, "not like his. I can't write at all, or do anything useful with mine."

"I'd hate to call what Roy does with his imagination useful to anyone—except Roy," Nicholas Hill said. "All the same, since you've obviously got imagination, I wonder if I could appeal to you to use it on something that hasn't been mentioned so far. I mean my sister-in-law, Sheila Hill. She's a widow and she lost her only child in a peculiarly horrible way. That's five years ago, and the wound's had a certain time to heal. It isn't fully healed—it never will be. But can't you imagine what dragging the whole story out into the light now is going to do to her?"

I could imagine it unpleasantly clearly and had been doing so from time to time ever since Bernard had first begun working on Teresa Swale. I had even made almost the same speech to Bernard that Nicholas Hill had just made to me and had been told rather sharply by Janet that as Bernard handled this sort of thing, nobody felt hurt, and, anyway, why didn't I mind my own business?

This should have made me sympathetic to Nicholas Hill, but instead it had the opposite effect. I felt that his attack on me was completely unfair. An accusation of blackmail, which I could have met honestly with injured innocence, would have been far less upsetting and infuriating than this one, in which I happened to be half on his side already.

I answered him rather nastily. "Do you mean that your sister-in-law actually reads *Alarum?*"

"It's unlikely," he said, "but the daily help probably does."

"Well, she's lucky to *have* daily help," I said, "and ought to realise that everything has its disadvantages. Personally I think it's far worse

43

to read a paper like *Alarum* than to write for it, because writing for it at least has the justification of keeping the wolf from the door."

I think if I had been talking only to Roy Carney, I might have gone on then and told him just how close the wolf had come to the door in Hampstead, how clearly we could hear the creature's snuffling under it. But I felt no impulse at all to make any appeal for sympathy to Nicholas Hill.

As it was, Roy Carney came to my help.

"Hear, hear," he said. "Don't take any notice of him, Miss Purvis. He had a gilded youth and doesn't understand some of the cold realities of life—one of which, of course, is hunger, from which I'm suffering rather badly at the moment. I arrived by plane from America this morning and that built-in clock we're all supposed to have inside us hasn't adjusted itself yet to that five-hour difference. So what about our all going on somewhere for a meal, which you can call an early dinner and I'll call a late lunch? Only let's have another drink first."

"Sorry, Roy, I can't stay," Nicholas Hill answered quickly, and another of those understanding glances passed between the two men, though it seemed to me this time that it was not nearly as friendly as I had thought before.

"All right, we'll do without you, Nick," Roy Carney said. "You'll keep me company though, won't you, Miss Purvis? I've been abroad for years and I'm practically a stranger. I need someone to look after me."

Refusing that invitation was the most difficult thing that I had done that day. Inside I was bursting with pleasure at having been asked to have dinner by Roy Carney. But there was Janet at home, probably feverishly wondering why I had not returned long ago, and there was the question of how Bernard was. So really there was no possibility at all of my saying anything but that I had already stayed too long and had come only to ask him, if he should hear anything of Teresa Swale, to let me know; so I left the Lincolns' telephone number and said good-bye.

I managed to do all this without letting regret bite into me too painfully, but a few minutes later, as I walked away towards Piccadilly, a black cloud of depression came down on my spirits. However nice he had been about it, I thought, he could not really want me to find Teresa Swale any more than his friend did. He would not use that telephone number and I should certainly never see him again.

"Miss Purvis," a voice said behind me.

Because of its deep note, I knew before I looked round that it was Nicholas Hill. He fell into step beside me and we walked on together. I waited for him to say what he had on his mind.

After a moment, he said, "I understand it's asking a great deal, but is there really no chance that that article could be withdrawn?"

"I doubt it," I said.

"I'm sorry if I was insulting about it—all the same, you under stand why I asked, don't you?"

"I do, as a matter of fact," I said unhappily.

"I rather thought you did," he said. "That's why I thought it might be worth trying again."

"But I've really no say in the matter, and besides . . ." I stopped. I was not going to start defending Bernard to him. Bernard was the nicest man I had ever known, and he did not need defending.

"There's another thing," Nicholas Hill went on. "When I said you might be getting into deep water, that could be true, you know."

"That sounds almost like a threat," I said.

"It's nothing of the sort," he said. "It's a warning. For your own good. There could be all sorts of reasons why Teresa Swale vanished just when she was expecting to have her life story published in *Alarum*. You ought to be able to think of some of them yourself and to realise that it might be best to steer clear of the whole business. Leave it to the *Alarum* people to track her down. But keep out of it yourself. Even five years later, the aftermath of an unsolved murder could be dangerous."

He turned and walked away.

I stood still for a moment, listening to the echoes of the words "an unsolved murder." All of a sudden I was overcome by a feeling that behind all the familiar things around me—the people going home from work or starting out for the evening, the busses, the taxis, the stolid entrance of Burlington House, the windows of Fortnum and Mason's—there was a darkness that I had never sensed before. A shiver of the same panic that had seized me in the squalid bed-sitting room of Callie Mars prickled along my spine.

It was a relief to see a policeman strolling towards me and to see that he, at any rate, seemed to find the scene calm and normal and the bright summer evening a pleasant one. Recovering, I walked to Piccadilly to catch a Number Thirteen bus home to Swiss Cottage.

I found Janet cooking a meal of lamb chops, mashed potatoes, spinach, and queen-of-puddings. She was concentrated and composed. She told me that the news of Bernard was at least no worse. When I told her how I had been spending my time, she did something unusual. She came to me and put her arms tightly round me. Then she went back to whipping up the meringue for the pudding. She ate hardly anything herself that evening, but I was hungry and finished everything she put before me.

Afterwards I settled down to reading the carbon copy of Bernard's manuscript, which I had been carrying around with me all day. As I expected, I found that the Hill family had very little to fear from what he had written about them, because, apart from the fact that he had a quite sensitive nature, Bernard understood the law of libel. There was less in his story about the short time that Teresa Swale had spent in the Hills' home than about her childhood and strict upbringing, while the main part of what he had written was devoted to what had happened to her after her acquittal, when the suspicion of her guilt had dogged her along her downward path.

There was no mention at all of Nicholas Hill and very little was said of the mother of the dead child, apart from a quotation from an interview that she had given to the press after the trial, when she had said that she personally had never had any doubt of Teresa's innocence.

Janet and I both went to bed early, and in the short time that I lay there quietly in the darkness before I fell asleep, I wondered if Nicholas Hill really believed that that death was an unsolved murder, or if he had simply thought that the word would frighten me off my search for Teresa. After all, no shadow of a motive had ever been suggested. No one else had ever been brought to trial. It looked as if the police had long ago written off as a blunder the verdict of murder given by the coroner's court, and had made up their minds that it should have been one of accidental death.

I found this somehow a comforting thought and my sleep was deep and dreamless.

Next day, when Janet set off to the hospital to see Bernard, I set off for Somerset House. Luckily for me, I found a very helpful clerk, but even so I was disappointed to find that there was no hope of obtaining Teresa's marriage certificate that day. The search for it, I was told, would be difficult, since I did not know her husband's name, and the document would have to be posted to me.

In fact, it was two days before the certificate came—two days of worry over Bernard, whose temperature remained so stubbornly high that Janet and I almost forgot Teresa. But at last, by the second post, the certificate arrived, and any peace of mind that I had been able to draw from the belief that the death of little David Hill had been a tragic accident and not a revolting and unavenged crime was abruptly destroyed. For I saw that in January of the year in which David Hill had died, Teresa had been married in a village in Cornwall to Nicholas Hill.

CHAPTER FIVE

Paddington Station was a mob of jostling, irritable humanity. The holiday season had begun, and although it was a Thursday, there were queues across the station for the trains to the Devonshire resorts. The train to Gloucester was crowded, and I had to stand in the corridor until the first stop. After that, I had a seat beween an oversized soldier, who kept various pieces of his equipment slung about him so that their corners stuck into my ribs, and a young mother with a wriggling two-year-old child on her lap.

She was fretful herself about the child's restlessness and kept talking to me. She told me he had just been seriously ill and in hospital as a result of swallowing an ice-lolly whole. The experience appeared to have left no trauma in the mind of the child, because when an older child passed along the corridor with the remains of an ice-lolly in one fist and a lot of sticky pinkness dripping from his chin, the infant lunged forward with both hands out, so that it nearly fell off its mother's lap, and shrieked with envy.

The conditions for thought were not favourable. I said thank you to someone who thrust a picture paper into my hands, and for the rest of the journey I read the comic strips and listened to the young mother scolding and praising, and apologizing for, her child.

Since Janet had been away at the hospital when I received Teresa's marriage certificate, I had left her a note, telling her what I had just learned about Nicholas Hill and that since the only clue to Teresa's whereabouts was her statement that she was going to get some money from her husband's family, I was going to Gloucestershire to see if I could find some trace of her there. I had then packed a bag, telephoned a friend of Janet's to ask her to call in later to see that Janet was all right, and left for Paddington.

In Gloucester I discovered that the village of Footfield was seven miles away and that the busses ran rather less than hourly. Over tea and sandwiches in the bus station, while I was waiting, I found I could think more calmly than in the train, but however calmly and however deeply I thought, I still could not imagine how it had been possible, during a murder investigation, for the police to have failed to discover that Teresa Swale had been married to a member of the Hill family.

At her trial the defence had made a great deal of her total lack of motive for the murder of the child, yet if the truth was that all the time she had been secretly married to a man who, she believed—possibly wrongly, unless there was some question of entail—would inherit his brother's fortune if the child could be got out of the way, she had had the most obvious and powerful of motives.

The lack of suspicion aroused by Nicholas Hill himself was also puzzling. In fact, he seemed not to have come into the story at all. Bernard had not even mentioned him, and in my own vague memories of the trial there was no one who could be fitted into the role of wicked uncle. I had a curiously vivid memory of David's photograph in the newspapers and also of his mother's, but the dark, striking face of the man whom I had seen the day before had seemed entirely unfamiliar.

And after the trial, what had happened? That he and Teresa had not dared to avow the marriage even after Teresa's acquittal was natural enough. But why had she apparently gained nothing by her crime? If Nicholas had successfully inherited a large sum of money through it, why was she living in poverty? Why wasn't she living comfortably on blackmail? Where had she, or both of them, miscalculated? By the time that the Footfield bus came into the bus station, the number of questions which I saw needed to be asked had multiplied.

I got off the bus twenty minutes later outside a pub called the Rose and Thorn. It was quite small but it had AA and RAC signs up, and as I saw no hope of returning to London that evening, the first thing I did was to go inside and book a room. Writing my name and address in the visitors' book, I looked to see if by any chance Teresa had registered before me. But that would have been too easy. There was no Swale and no Hill.

I thought of asking the manageress about her, but instead only asked, as she took me up to my room, if she could tell me where Footfield House was.

She was a small, faded woman in a navy blue and white dress that drooped around the hem. She gave me a curious look, beckoned me to the window, and pointed along the road.

"Take that turning just before you get to the church," she said, "and it's the old house with the white gates—you can't miss it. But you're too late if you're thinking of buying it. Well, dinner any time between seven and eight. We can't do it later than that, me being almost singlehanded, but we'll do our best for you."

She went out and closed the door, leaving me with a very bothersome suspicion in my mind. To settle it, I went out immediately without waiting to unpack, or even to have a wash. I walked along the village street between cottages built of that beautiful stone which always has a soft golden warmth in its greyness. Most of the cottages were thatched, and their gardens were bright with roses, pinks, and sweet peas growing comfortably amongst the lettuces and French beans. The evening sunshine made all the colours luminous, and here and there, trapped in the reflection from a window, it became a fire on the glass. I took the turning just before the church. It was an ancient church, with a square tower, standing among yews and old gravestones. I walked a little way down this turning and then saw a long, low stone house with big white gates in front of it. The gates stood open. But one glance at the unwashed, uncurtained windows, at the peeling paint and the overgrown garden told me that my suspicion had been correct. Footfield House had not been lived in for years.

As I turned back to the Rose and Thorn, I was extremely angry with myself. What an incredibly stupid assumption it had been that Mrs. Hill would have lived on alone in Footfield after the death of her child. She probably lived in London, or Bournemouth, or abroad, and if only I had stopped to think, I could have saved myself this pointless journey.

Over dinner, at which the manageress and I were the only people eating in the little dark dining room, we kept up a conversation from our separate tables. I asked her how long the house had stood empty.

"Oh, I could've told you that if I'd known what you wanted," she said. "It's been up for sale for years and now it's been bought by someone in London and it's going to be turned into a country club. There was a gentleman here to lunch today who somebody said was the new owner. The change'll hit us, though of course we'll keep the local trade, because the village people won't want anything as grand as that; but I don't know if we'll do as well as we do now with meals, and it may get even harder to get labour."

"Did you know Mrs. Hill?" I asked.

"No, she was gone before I ever got here," the manageress answered. "I've only been here four years and she went away right after the tragedy. Moved away and never came back, which is what I'd have done in her place."

"Do you know where she moved to?" I asked.

"No, I couldn't say," she said. "She didn't belong here herself and she hadn't lived here long and the village people hadn't seen much of her." For the first time she seemed to think that there was something in my arrival and my curiosity that needed explaining. "Is there any special reason . . . ?" she asked and paused delicately.

"Yes, I'm a journalist and I'm doing a series of articles on well-known murders, ancient and modern," I said. "This one isn't very well known, but it has some very interesting features."

"I thought in the end they decided it wasn't a murder," she said. "That girl got off, didn't she?"

"I should have said murder trials," I said. "That's what's so interesting about it. At the time everyone was so certain it was murder, and then it all fizzled out."

"Oh well, if you knew village people as well as I do!" she said and shrugged her shoulders. "They like something to talk about. I think myself it was just an accident. Still, I see what you mean. It *is* interesting, when you come to think of it. That's what comes of having an imagination. I expect you're very clever. I never know how people think of all the things to write about they do. I'm sure I never could. What paper d'you write for, Miss Purvis?"

"Oh, I'm just a free-lance; I sell things wherever I can," I said. "Do you know if there's anyone in the village who could tell me where Mrs. Hill moved to?"

"Well, like I said, she didn't belong here and she wasn't here long enough to make friends," she answered. "I couldn't tell you if she still writes to anyone here—the vicar, perhaps. Of course, there's Mrs. Bullock."

The name sounded familiar, and I thought that Bernard must have mentioned it in speaking of the case, though it was not in his manuscript. I asked who she was.

"She was housekeeper at Footfield House at the time," the manageress said. "She was with the family for years before the Colonel married, and she used to keep the house going while he was abroad. She lives in the cottage just beyond it—the one with the pale blue door and the window boxes. It used to be the gardener's cottage, I believe, and the Hills gave it to her when they shut up the house, and it's all done up very nice now, because her son's done well for himself and sends her money. Or that's what some people say. Some people say the Hills pay her a pension. She isn't much of a talker and she'd never talk about their affairs, which is as it should be. She speaks to everyone in a friendly way and she's very well thought of, but she doesn't talk."

"Do you think she'd mind if I called on her this evening?" I asked.

"I don't see why she should," she answered.

So after I had finished my roast chicken and plum pie and custard, I took another walk through the village. But when I found myself standing opposite the big white gates in front of the desolate, old house, I paused. I thought that I could identify the spot from which David Hill had fallen. It was said that the pink flowers of a clematis had drawn him to the window, and there was one window on the first floor which was half hidden by a thick cushion of the reddish leaves of *montana rubens*. In May it would be a starry mass of flowers, as bright and lovely as ever. I stared at it with a sickened sort of fascination, as if the plant bore some unexpiated guilt for the tragedy.

And between me and the house there was the hedge which, by concealing David's body from the road, had also played a part in the story. The hedge was of yew, which had sprouted raggedly and now was so tall that it almost hid the lower-floor windows. In the evening light, which was not yet quite twilight but had lost the clarity of day, the darkness of the yew looked sinister. And there is always something eerie about a deserted house and neglected garden. That was why, I suppose, my heart suddenly raced when I heard footsteps on the other side of the hedge.

They were firm, rapid footsteps, and they were going towards the gate. Shaking off the spell of the place, I realised that they probably belonged to a caretaker or perhaps to the new owner, who had lunched that day at the Rose and Thorn and who was going to turn Footfield House into a country club and who would almost certainly pull down the rioting clematis and trim the yew into shapes of peacocks and pigeons. There was no reason for me to linger to see who it was.

Yet I did, and I saw a stocky, grey-haired man, who wore a good tweed suit and carried a leather brief case, come out of the gate and walk quickly along the road towards a cottage that had a pale blue door and window boxes full of geraniums. He knocked and was admitted.

Since Mrs. Bullock had a visitor, I changed my mind about going to see her and, strolling back to the Rose and Thorn, asked the manageress if I could use the telephone.

I rang up Janet. When she answered, she sounded flustered and half angry and said that she could not imagine why I had gone rushing off like that without waiting to discuss the matter first with her.

I told her I wished that I had not, though it had seemed the obvious thing to do at the time. I could not say much more than that, because the telephone was in a passage, with the door into the bar only a yard away. I asked her about Bernard and she said that at last his temperature had started to go down. I asked her how she was feeling herself and she answered shortly that she was quite all right.

"But are you all right, Elspeth?" she asked. "I've been feeling terrible about you all day. I feel I've got you into something which you shouldn't really be mixed up with at all. You're too young, and the sort of people you've been seeing . . . Well, I know at your age everyone pretends to be hard-boiled, but I happen to know you aren't, and so does Bernard. He'll never forgive me when he finds out about it. Promise me you'll come straight home tomorrow."

"There's someone I want to see first," I said.

"Who?" she asked.

I did not want to say the name aloud in that passage. "Someone who may be able to tell me something I want to know," I answered.

"Oh dear," she said fretfully, "I do wish you'd just come home. I'm blaming myself most frightfully. I know it's all because I worried you about the money, but we'll manage somehow—we always have. So please just come home, Elspeth."

"Well, with luck I'll be home by lunch time tomorrow or soon after," I said. "As it happens, I'm really rather enjoying myself."

"That's what I was afraid of," she said. "That's why I feel so responsible. Anyway, I hope you *don't* find Teresa. I've been sitting here remembering that horrible voice of hers and feeling more and more certain she murdered that poor child, and I hope most sincerely you don't manage to catch up with her."

I promised to telephone again if there were any unexpected developments; then we said good night to one another and I went up to bed.

I had breakfast early next morning, and immediately after it I set out to see Mrs. Bullock, hoping that she would not object too much to an early visitor. My knock on the pale blue door with the gleaming knocker brought answering footsteps at once. It was almost as if I had been expected, and the feeling that I *had* been persisted even when Mrs. Bullock opened the door and gave me a blank look and an enquiring, "Good morning."

This was because, as I met her grey eyes, I had an immediate feeling of recognition. I knew that I had never seen her before and yet I felt just as if I had. It was disconcerting, even though a possible explanation of it was that I had seen her photograph in the newspapers five years before and ever since had carried around a faint memory of her features.

She was a short woman, about sixty years old, broad in the shoulders and the hips, and heavy in the bosom. Under a white cotton dress with black spots her whole short body had a monolithic rigidity. She had thick grey hair, parted in the middle and bound in plaits across the top of her head. Her face was square and flat with a small nose, a small, neat mouth, ruddy cheeks, and remarkably few wrinkles.

I told her my name and said that I had been told that she might be able to tell me the present address of Mrs. Hill.

She frowned, but I saw no surprise on her face. After a moment, she said, "Well, come in, Miss Purvis."

Moving to one side, she let me in and closed the door behind me. As soon as I entered, I knew why Mrs. Bullock had looked familiar, for, smiling cheerfully out of a silver frame in a place of honour on top of a mahogany bureau, was a photograph of Roy Carney, and he and Mrs. Bullock were so like one another that they could only be mother and son.

CHAPTER SIX

She saw my startled look and a gleam of satisfaction lit up her inexpressive grey eyes.

"Yes, that's my boy," she said. "It's good of him, too, though it was taken a few years ago. You know his books, I expect. He's been getting on very well, getting quite famous."

"Then his name isn't really Carney," I said.

We had both sat down on little, cretonne-covered chairs. Mrs. Bullock sat with her feet, in their black slippers and grey cotton stockings, planted parallel, about nine inches apart on a homemade rug. Her broad hands, with a wedding ring deeply embedded in the flesh of one short finger, were folded in her lap.

"No, he just made that up, like writers do—I couldn't say why," she said. Her voice was calm and flat and her lips hardly moved as she talked. "His name isn't Roy either; it's Billie."

"You must be very proud of him," I said.

"Well, I don't know about proud," she answered in a restrained voice, though her pride was in every inch of her. "He's done better than I expected. He was a scamp when he was a boy. He'd never

56

stick at anything. But he works hard at his writing, there's no question of that. I suppose it's what he was meant to do all along, though I used to want him to be a doctor. Colonel Hill always said he'd see him through the university, only Billie always failed his exams. He'd never work at anything he didn't like. Still, it's all been for the best in the end, because he's making much more money than he could've made at his age as a doctor. He's much richer now than Mr. Nicholas, who's an architect. That still seems strange to me, remembering them as boys together, when it was Mr. Nicholas who had the prospects. But they're still great friends, Billie tells me. He's very loyal, Billie is. He'd never let a friend down."

"It's strange that you haven't any of his books in your room," I said.

"Well, books collect dust, and, too, I don't care for showing off," she said. "There aren't many people here who know just what he does. I shouldn't have mentioned it to you if I hadn't seen you recognised his photo."

"I suppose he and Mr. Hill have known each other most of their lives," I said.

"Well, since they were about ten," she said. "I remember Billie'd just had his tenth birthday when we came here. I took the job because of the raids and thinking I'd like to get Billie away from London. The Colonel was away in Singapore and got taken prisoner by the Japs and we never saw him till after the war. Mrs. Hill—I mean his mother, not his wife—was alone here with Mr. Nicholas, and she was in poor health already and I looked after her and Mr. Nicholas when he wasn't away at his boarding school, and of course he and Billie became fast friends. We only used one end of the house, because the rest had been taken over by a girls' school, and I didn't have any help and did all the cooking and shopping and everything by myself. But Mrs. Hill wasn't any trouble, poor soul, and she was very kind to Billie, and so was the Colonel when he came back, and I stayed on and ran the house for him, though we'd one or two other servants then, and I kept it going for him when he went abroad again and when he married. And I was still here when young Mrs. Hill came home without him, and I helped her look after little David until . . . Well, until she went away. So you see, Footfield House was really Billie's home, and that's something he'll never forget, and he'll always stand by Mr. Nicholas."

Something in her story had worried me. There was something in it that did not fit with what I knew, or thought that I knew, about her son. But for the moment I could not put my finger on what it was.

"Can you tell me where Mrs. Hill lives now?" I asked. "That's what I really came to ask you."

"She went back to Scotland," Mrs. Bullock answered. "She's a Scotch lady, and after the tragedy she went home to her own people. I've got her address written down somewhere. I still get a card from her at Christmas, but she isn't much of a one for writing letters."

Standing up, she crossed to the mahogany bureau and opened the flap. From one of the pigeonholes inside she brought out a handful of Christmas cards. Whether she always kept all the Christmas cards that she received, or only the ones which she found particularly artistic, I do not know, but after a moment she extracted one with a picture of Edinburgh Castle on it and handed it to me. Inside there were a few lines of greeting and inquiries after Mrs. Bullock's health written in a small, neat handwriting and signed with the name, Sheila Hill. An address in Edinburgh was written underneath it.

"You may as well keep the card," Mrs. Bullock said. "I know I've got a note of the address somewhere else and I'm not likely to need it, anyway. I can't say letter writing's much in my line, any more than it is in hers. I don't know where Billie gets his writing from, because his father wasn't a clever man at all and just about knew how to fill in his football coupons. But I'd a grandfather who was a minister, so perhaps that's where it comes from."

The flat voice stopped. I thanked her and put the card away in my handbag.

"Do you know if there are any other Hills?" I asked. "Any uncles or aunts or cousins?"

"Not that I ever heard of," Mrs. Bullock said. "There's just young Mrs. Hill and Mr. Nicholas. He lives in London and you can find his address if you want it in the phone book. I haven't seen him since they left the house. Neither of them wanted to live here, and I don't suppose, with death duties and income tax and all, there's really the money left to keep the place up. I'd have liked Billie to buy it, having a sort of feeling for the place myself, but he's settled in Hollywood and says what would he want with a place that size anyway, which is quite true. So there you are."

"And Teresa Swale," I said. "You haven't by any chance seen anything of her recently, have you?"

For the first time she showed emotion. A dark flush, which began inside the V neck of her spotted cotton dress and mounted up her throat, spread over her cheeks and forehead. When she spoke, her voice was shaking.

"She'd better not let me! That woman! I warned Mrs. Hill, I told her what she was, but she wouldn't listen. And now I couldn't answer for myself if I set eyes on her. And she knows it, too—oh no, she won't come near me!"

The anger of another person is a disturbing thing, even when it is not directed against oneself. It was in that little room that I felt for the first time a breath, not only of the tragedy, but of the violence that had shattered the lives of the Hills. Standing up, I thanked Mrs. Bullock again and started to wend my way in and out between her belongings to the door. Her face was still red with the violence of her feelings and her small mouth tight and hard as she followed me and closed the door behind me.

I was half way back to the Rose and Thorn before it occurred to me that she had shown a rather odd lack of curiosity about my visit. So far as I could remember, she had not asked a single question about the reasons for my interest in the Hills.

In the train back to London, I did some hard thinking about the interview with Mrs. Bullock. I thought about my feeling that there had been something wrong with her account of the Hill household and, after a time, I arrived at some conclusions that I did not like. I did not like them in part because it seemed to me they meant that certain people had not been taking me seriously. Usually this is not a thing that I mind particularly, but on this occasion it made me hot with anger. I was in a very bad temper when, at about half past two, I arrived back at the flat in Hampstead, let myself in at the front door, and heard Janet laughing in answer to something said in a man's voice.

It was the last voice, as it happened, that I wanted to hear just then. I felt my cheeks flushing as I went to the sitting room.

Roy Carney was sitting over coffee with Janet. There was a brightness in her face that had not been there for the last few days, and I saw that they had been having lunch together. The remains of some salad and biscuits and cheese were still on the table. So were some empty sherry glasses and a beer mug.

He sprang to his feet as I came in. There was a sparkle of amusement in his grey eyes and a not quite convincing note of apology in his voice as he said, "I could have told you! If only you'd told me what you were thinking of doing, I could have told you it was no use going to Footfield."

"You knew I was going without my telling you," I said.

"How could I possibly have done that?" he asked.

"Your mother was expecting me," I said. "Wasn't that because you'd told her to?"

"Mr. Carney found out where you'd gone from me," Janet said. "He rang up this morning and wanted to speak to you, so I told him about your going to look for Teresa in Footfield."

"His name isn't Carney," I said. "It's Bullock—Billie Bullock."

He grinned and said, "You must have got on well with my mother if she told you that. She usually doesn't own me."

"You told her to tell me," I said. "You rang her up and told her to expect me and to answer all my questions."

He scratched his head. "I didn't exactly. But even if I had, what would have been wrong with that?"

"I'm not sure; that's what's worrying me," I said. "There's something all wrong about it, but I can't make out what it is."

He gave me a serious look, then looked at Janet and cocked a pale eyebrow at her. "I'm in bad, but I don't know what I've done—do you?" His tone was flippant, but there was a note of anxiety behind it.

"I expect she's tired—or hungry. That always upsets her temper," Janet said, giving me an elder sister's look.

"I'm tired *and* hungry," I said. "But what's really inducing this mood of rancour is the thought of how Billie-boy and his friend talked to me the other evening, as if they didn't realise I was serious about meaning to find Teresa. First they tried to make a fool of me by telling me a lot of nonsense. Then they tried to frighten me off. And now—now I'm not sure what they're up to."

I saw a dull red mount in Roy's tanned cheeks.

"You rather took us by surprise, you know," he said. "But I can't remember saying anything frightening. An invitation to dinner isn't usually considered a threat."

"I rather thought your friend's parting remarks to me were meant to sound like a threat," I said.

"I can't remember what they were," he said. "Something about what opening up the whole subject of the murder might do to his sister-in-law. I thought it was all quite moderate for Nick, who can sometimes go off the deep end rather badly."

"I meant what he said when he followed me out," I said.

"I don't know what he said then."

"He told me it might be dangerous to get mixed up in an unsolved murder case."

I saw a flicker in his eyes as if this were news to him. But before he could say anything, Janet exclaimed, "That's what I've been thinking more and more myself. I could hardly sleep, thinking of Elspeth chasing around after that awful woman. Don't worry, Mr. Carney. I'm going to see that she drops it."

"I'm going to find Teresa if it's the last thing I do," I said. "I'm going to find her and make her sign that paper for Bernard."

The amusement had gone from Roy Carney's face. For a moment it looked as empty and expressionless as his mother's. Then it slowly relaxed again and he turned to Janet with a smile.

"Well, thanks very much for the lunch, Mrs. Lincoln," he said. "I hope we'll meet again sometime in a less tense atmosphere."

He held out a hand and Janet took it, flushing with embarrassment. As he picked up a brief case from a chair and went out, she hurried after him and I heard her trying to chatter conversationally as she saw him out.

When she came back, she said explosively, "Elspeth—to make a scene like that—whatever got into you?"

"What did he really come for?" I asked.

"I think he just wanted to see you," she answered.

"No, that can't have been it," I said.

"Why not? He rang up quite early this morning and wanted to speak to you, so I told him where you'd gone and that you'd said you'd probably be home by lunch time, and he asked if he could come out to see you."

"Did you tell him about our finding out about Teresa being married to Nicholas Hill?"

"I never said anything about it at all. Actually we hardly talked about Teresa. We talked about quite ordinary things. I thought he was very charming and amusing. He told me about some of his experiences in Intelligence during the war and they were extraordinarily interesting. He must be rather older than he looks. He really looks amazingly young, doesn't he?"

"Listen," I said furiously, "when the war ended he was fifteen years old. His mother told me that. She took him to Footfield because of the bombing, and he'd just had his tenth birthday. I knew there was something the matter with it when she told me that, but I couldn't think straight away what it was; but in the train I remembered the story he'd told me about a spy called Leni Briefbach, and the simple truth is that unless they run a juvenile branch in Intelligence, which is something I've never heard of, that whole story was a lie from start to finish."

Janet gave me a bewildered look. "But what was the point of it?"

"I don't know what the point was of what he told you," I said. "The point of what he told me was that it was supposed to get my mind off Teresa. I don't know what good he thought it would do, and I don't think Nicholas Hill did either, because he suddenly banged his

62

glass on the table to make Roy shut up, then had a go at appealing to my better nature. And when that didn't work, Roy asked me out to dinner, hoping that charm would do it. And when that didn't work, Nicholas came after me and threatened me. And they couldn't tell whether or not that had worked, so Roy rang you up to find out—and you told him I'd gone to Footfield. So they knew it hadn't worked. And then comes the bit I can't understand. Roy rang up his mother—he must have—and told her to expect me and to answer my questions. But why did he do that? That's been worrying me all the way back to London."

"He said he hadn't done exactly that," Janet said in a tone of unhappy protest.

"He *said!* He's a liar, Janet, a fluent liar. And I was told in the village that Mrs. Bullock didn't go in for gossiping about the Hills, and she really can't be a gossip, because apparently she's never let on that she's the mother of Roy Carney. Yet when I walked in on her, a perfect stranger, she told me every single thing I wanted to know. And I'm sure that was only because he'd told her to. But what I can't understand is—why did he do that?"

"D'you know something!" Janet said. "I think you've just lost your temper with him because he pulled your leg about being in Intelligence. Personally, I rather respect him for it. As he said, you took him by surprise and he just talked away to try to cover up for his friend. Even if what he said did come out of one of his own books, I think it was very loyal. And I think you laid on the abominably embarrassing scene that you did just now out of wounded vanity. You couldn't forgive him for your own idea that that invitation to dinner didn't come out of simple yearning for your company."

I stood up, picked up a book that happened to be lying on the arm of a chair, and brought it down with a crash on the table. It did not really express what I felt, but there was some satisfaction in it.

"Anyway, I'm going to Edinburgh," I said.

"No, Elspeth!" Janet cried.

"I'll go tonight," I said.

"That's absolutely impossible."

"Why?" I asked.

"For one thing, it's too expensive. I haven't that much money in the house and it's too late to go to the bank."

"I went to the bank on my way home and cashed some of my own money," I said.

"But we couldn't let you use your own on doing something like this for us," she said.

"Look, if Bernard ever gets that thousand pounds, I'll send in a bill for expenses," I said. "Meanwhile, I'm going to Edinburgh."

Janet sighed helplessly and said, "Bernard'll be furious when he hears about it."

"He won't, you know," I said. "He'll be interested and excited. How is he, Janet?"

"*Much* better," she said, her face brightening. "His temperature's almost down to normal, although he's horribly weak. They aren't going to let him come home for some days, and he'll have to go very slow even when they do send him back. But the worst's over and there's nothing to worry about any more."

"Well, he'll recover twice as fast if he hasn't got financial worries," I said. "So I'll go to Edinburgh. And if Teresa's been anywhere near Mrs. Hill, I'll track her down. Don't try to stop me, Janet. This thing's got into me. I couldn't drop it now if I tried."

"It's never been much good trying to stop you doing something you've really made up your mind to do," she said with another sigh. "But I don't like you spending your own money on it. There can't be much of it."

"There's enough for that. And think of that lavish salary that starts in September."

She smiled. "You know, it *will* feel lavish for a few weeks. The first money you earn always seems limitless. But then you'll start feeling poor like the rest of us. What train are you thinking of taking?"

"There's one at ten-forty," I said. "I did think of flying, but it's more expensive and I'd get there too late this evening to do anything much, so if I travel overnight I shan't actually lose much time. And there's something I want to do before I leave. I want to play those tapes over again, or as much of them as I've time for. You see, there's

64

something in this whole situation that I can't understand at all. The story Bernard's written up doesn't even touch it. But of course he was deliberately bringing in the Hills as little as he could. The thing is, why didn't the police get on to the marriage between Teresa and Nicholas? Why isn't he even mentioned in the story? Billie Bullock isn't mentioned either, but that isn't really so odd, because he isn't a member of the family. But being married to Nicholas gave Teresa an obvious motive for killing that child. David was the sole descendant of the elder brother, the one Mrs. Bullock calls the Colonel. So the house and all the family property would have gone to David and there wouldn't have been much for Nicholas. But if David could be got rid of, that would have changed, wouldn't it? Nicholas would have inherited. So why didn't that marriage come to light? Why didn't Nicholas come into the story?"

"When it came to the point, there doesn't seem to have been much to inherit," Janet said. "And anyway, wouldn't the Colonel have left most of it to his wife?"

"Teresa mightn't have known that. Even Nicholas may not have known it. Because the family was rich once, they may have thought there was still lots of money left. So now I'm going to play those tapes over again to see if Teresa ever said anything about Nicholas that Bernard left out. There may be something there, some hint she dropped accidentally, that'll throw a little light on the problem."

Janet gave a groan and said, "Those tapes again! That voice!"

But she sounded more interested and she followed me to the door as I went into Bernard's room.

I took two steps into the little room, then stood still.

"Janet, you haven't put those tapes away anywhere, have you?" I asked.

"I don't think I've even been in here since Bernard got ill," she answered.

"But you did leave Roy Carney alone in the sitting room."

"Yes, of course I did, when I went to get lunch."

"Well, now we know what he really came for," I said. "And we know why he brought a brief case with him. He's taken the tapes away with him—the whole lot of them."

CHAPTER SEVEN

At first Janet was angry. This was at the idea that anyone could dare to interfere with Bernard's property. But then the spell that Roy Carney had cast upon her regained its power and she began to say that his loyalty to his friend was really quite impressive, was most unusual, was something to admire.

I said disgustedly, "Oh, they're in cahoots all right. They grew up like twin brothers and one always picks up where the other leaves off."

I thought of going straight out after Roy to accuse him of the theft and to get the tapes back, but then realised that he would be prepared for precisely that, and so would probably not have gone back to his hotel. I might easily waste the rest of the day in trying to track him down. Giving up the idea of following him, I set about repacking my bag for my journey to Scotland. A tweed suit, I thought, a mackintosh and a spare jumper and skirt would be more sensible wear than the summer dress that I had taken to Footfield.

I was intending to leave for King's Cross by bus, but Janet insisted on standing me a taxi. So I arrived at the station with time to spare, bought my ticket, and, before the train really started to fill, settled down in the corner of an empty second-class compartment. I won-dered if by any chance I should have the luck to keep the whole seat to myself and be able to lie down and sleep. But Friday evening is a busy time for travelling and before the train started a young couple, a middle-aged woman, and an elderly man joined me and I reconciled myself to sitting up all night.

As the train slid out of the station, I started to read a thriller that I had borrowed from Janet. But as the train gathered speed in the deepening darkness, in which presently, after London had been left behind, there were only the clustered lights of one small town after another, strung along the railway, I let the book sink onto my lap and sat staring absently through the pale reflections on the glass be-side me at the blackness behind them. I had chosen that time, I do not know why, to start thinking about my future.

I did not often think about the future. It seemed a thing that I could always put off. I did a fair amount of dreaming, but that was different, and I do not think that I often deceived myself that it was not. The real future had a way of presenting one from time to time with events which were to be seen looming up for so long that it almost seemed impossible to believe that they could ever really hap-pen. Such, through the years of school, had been the day when I should leave it. I had felt that that day could never really arrive, yet suddenly there it was, and then it was behind me. Even more startling, in some ways, because of the way that the adult world had loomed up beyond it, had been the day when I realised that I had some rather insignificant letters after my name and that the doors of the university had closed and would not reopen. And now, ahead of me, was the job of which I had often talked with what I had assumed was enthusiasm, but which I had recently come to realise I had never thought seriously about at all. It was obvious that I did not know what I wanted and that I had a great deal to learn about myself. Meanwhile, like it or not, there was that job to be faced in September. And it would be as well to make up my mind to like it, since I did not seem able to make up my mind to turn my back on it.

But as I sat in the train, listening to the rhythm of the wheels, always so much more insistent at night than in the daytime, my drowsy mind would not take a firm hold on any good intentions. A face, a voice kept getting in the way. I scorned myself for it, but I could not stop thinking about Roy Carney.

I thought about the lies that he had told both Janet and me and about his theft of the tapes. I thought also about the fact that, unless I had quite misunderstood them, all his actions seemed to have sprung out of loyalty to Nicholas Hill. All the same, could you ever trust a man who seemed not quite to know the point where fact and fantasy blended?

At some point in the midst of this self-questioning I must have fallen asleep, for presently I found myself about to take an examination which I knew was of the greatest importance, yet I didn't know whether or not I had paid the entrance fee. So all my hard work was possibly going to be for nothing. It was one of those dreams that are extraordinarily distressing without exactly being a nightmare, and it was a relief to be jolted awake by the train's stopping at Grantham. The elderly man and the middle-aged woman both got out there, leaving the whole of the opposite seat empty.

I was thinking of grabbing it and lying down, but the young wife got there first and stretched out in comfort with her husband's coat folded under her head as a pillow. But just after the train had started again, a man came down the dimly lit corridor and, with an apology for disturbing the girl, made for the corner seat facing me, so she had to sit up again, and this gave me a faint feeling of satisfaction. But the satisfaction went out like a match in a sharp draught when I realised that the man was Nicholas Hill.

When he saw that I had recognized him, he muttered, "Good evening." But he seemed inclined to settle himself as comfortably as possible and go to sleep, rather than to talk.

I sat and stared at him. Before I was ready to pretend to go to sleep again, there was something I had to say. I leant forward.

"Have you been following me?" I asked.

"Not following—just keeping a watch out," he answered.

"I don't understand," I said.

"At King's Cross," he said. "The trains to Edinburgh. Roy told me he thought you were getting ready to take off for Edinburgh this evening. So I waited around till I saw you."

"He had a fruitful morning, didn't he?" I said bitterly.

"I'm sorry about that," he said. "Don't worry, though, you'll get the tapes back."

"With suitable bits scrubbed off? Anyway, what's the point of following me?"

"In a general way, just to keep an eye on you, for your own good as well as several other people's," he said. "Roy told me you wouldn't give up the search for Teresa. He said you were a desperate character."

"Oh, he did? Well, suppose I'd gone by plane—what would you have done then?"

"Roy's covering London Airport."

I burst out laughing.

"Oh, I hope he has a long, cold wait!" I said.

Nicholas shook his head. "He'll be holed up comfortably somewhere—trust Roy."

"Anyway, how is it you can find the time?" I asked. "I thought you were an architect. Doesn't that mean you work in an office?"

"Not on a Saturday," he said. "I can dog your footsteps until the last train on Sunday—or, rather, the first plane on Monday morning."

A sigh, resentful because of our talking, reached us from the other end of the compartment. We exchanged shrugs and each settled back silently into his own corner. Nicholas closed his eyes and I went back to staring at the darkness outside the window.

I thought about the man opposite me and that marriage certificate and the puzzle of why it had never been discovered. Could it be, I wondered, that the police force was really corrupt and that someone had been well bribed to keep Nicholas out of the case? Did that explain why the Hills now seemed to have so little money?

This was the sort of idea that at one in the morning can become entirely convincing—the whole dark world turning into a chill and

69

sinister place in which no one is what he seems and no one is to be trusted. But to gain any real hold on my imagination, this idea would have had to upset the habit of mind of a lifetime. A slightly idiotic trust in the integrity of almost all policemen was as deeply ingrained in me as the habit of standing up when I heard the national anthem. Yet when I thought about going to the police with the information that I possessed about Nicholas Hill, I rejected the idea.

Just why I shrank from it as I did I could not have said. Perhaps it was mainly because it was something that I had never done before. I had never even been inside a police station. I should not know whom to ask for. I should not know how to begin. At the mere thought of attempting it, I was overwhelmed with self-consciousness.

Also, of course, there was the feeling that until I had Teresa's signature on Bernard's piece of paper, the less said to anyone the better. Yet there was something else as well, which made me turn my head and take a long look at the man slumped in the corner facing me, with his head nodding forward onto his chest and his eyes shut. He appeared to be asleep, and sleep had smoothed the nervous lines out of his face, taken years from it, and left it unguarded.

Suppose, I thought, he had been Teresa's victim, not the instigator of her crime, nor even her passive accomplice. And if he hadn't spoken up against her afterwards, they were, it had to be remembered, man and wife. No one could force him to bear witness against his wife, could he? I was a little hazy about just how that worked, but I thought that there was some law which would have let him out. And he did not look like a murderer, did he?

But just then my steady stare seemed to disturb him and he stirred and opened his eyes and suddenly I wasn't so sure. How could I tell what murderers look like? Can even a murderer recognise another murderer? Closing my own eyes, I tried to find a comfortable spot to rest my head, and at last succeeded in sleeping a little.

With the dawn, which came earlier than I had expected, because of the distance northward that we had travelled through the hours of darkness, I woke and knew that there would be no more sleep for me. Creeping out of the compartment and down the corridor, I had a wash, put on fresh powder and lipstick, combed my hair, then, instead of going back to my seat, stayed standing in the corridor, trying to work the cramp out of my muscles.

It was that strange moment when trees and rivers and sleeping houses have their own shapes again, instead of being part of an ambiguous pattern of shadows, but the light is of a rare, faint purple which is never to be seen at any other time. In this light, which sometimes lasts only for a few minutes, nothing seems quite itself. Secret things seem to be stirring and preparing to emerge from behind the familiar forms. Then the light grows stronger and the hinted promise of a revelation turns out to have been a misunderstanding, and it seems natural to forget the moment because it has so little to do with life.

I saw this dawn light shining on flat fields dotted with farmhouses, and they were still under its spell when Nicholas came to stand beside me in the corridor.

He did not speak to me, but also stood looking out of the window, and only a moment later we saw that, as if by some trick when we had not been looking, although we had never turned our eyes away, the sky had turned blue and we were back in ordinary daylight once more, a daylight touched with sunshine and very clear and clean, but in which the business of living went on.

It no longer felt natural to stand there without saying anything, so I said, "I suppose we're in Scotland now."

"No, we haven't even got to Newcastle yet," he answered.

"Well, you don't need to keep an eye on me," I said. "I'm not going to run out on you."

He stretched, rumpled his dark hair, and yawned. "I was just a bit afraid of it."

"I just didn't feel like sitting still any longer," I said.

"Well, I wish you'd chosen a more comfortable time for travelling."

"It was your idea, not mine, that you had to come, too."

His heavy eyebrows came together in a frown. "If only I understood just what you mean to do in Edinburgh."

71

"You know what I mean to do in Edinburgh."

"Roy thinks he knows. I'm not sure that he's right."

"I want to find Teresa Swale," I said. "I want her signature on a paper which states that she agrees to *Alarum* publishing my brother-in-law's story under her name. I want to get that as quickly as possible. Then I want to go home."

"Why do you think you'll find Teresa in Edinburgh?"

He was looking straight at me. There was no friendliness in his eyes, but only a wary intentness, as if he were concentrating on catching the slightest change of expression on my face.

I began, "Because the only clue I've got . . ." Then my voice dried up.

I had been going to say that the only clue I had was Teresa's statement to Callie Mars that she was going to get some money from her husband's family. But to have said that would have been exactly the same as telling him that I knew about the marriage that had been so remarkably hushed up, and suddenly I was afraid to do so.

It was a curious kind of fear. It was not a physical fear. It was not a fear that he would clap a hand over my mouth, open a door, and push me off the train. It was fear of what it would feel like to go on looking into his face after I had virtually accused him of being at least an accomplice in a peculiarly loathsome murder.

I do not think I had ever in my life had to accuse anyone of anything worse than giving me change for two shillings when I had handed over half a crown, and in doing even that I had always wrapped it up in layer on layer of politeness and been more than half ready to believe that it was I who was making the mistake and that actually it was only two shillings that I had handed over.

But how could you wrap up an accusation of murder in politeness? And once the words were out, how could the world ever be the same again? An ordinary sort of man, standing beside me in the corridor of an ordinary sort of train, would have been transformed into a monster and could never be changed back, and somehow it would have been my words that would have brought this about. I shrank from speaking, as if there would be a sort of guilt in doing so.

After a moment, Nicholas turned his head away and looked out again at the scene slipping rapidly by, quiet in the light of the early morning. Then he thrust a cigarette into his mouth, lit it, and smoked in short, angry puffs. I had not fooled him. He knew what I knew. But when it came to the point, he did not want to talk about it either.

Presently he said, "Is there no way of persuading you to keep away from Sheila?"

"Find Teresa for me," I said. "Then there'd be no need at all for me to bother Mrs. Hill."

"It may surprise you, but I would if I could," he said. "Things having gone so far, finding Teresa would be about the best thing I could do. However, I don't think we'll find her in Edinburgh. But we can always try. You can count on my co-operation. What's the first step you have in mind?"

"Breakfast," I said.

"Well, there are times when we seem to view things from the same angle."

"Rather a lot of breakfast."

"That's good," he said. "Food's a healthy taste. Healthier than most of your other tastes."

"What do you know about my other tastes?"

"I was thinking of this taste you seem to have for dashing about from place to place without adequate reason."

"My reason seems adequate to me."

At that point he dropped the attempt to keep up a conversation and, after a little while, we went back to our seats. Opening the thriller, of which I had got through only two chapters, I settled down to read.

At Newcastle, Nicholas fetched us both tea in paper mugs from a trolley on the platform, and I thanked him; then we relapsed into our silence again. My reading was not a success, so I gave it up and took to staring out of the window. I thought about Roy Carney's arrival in England just then, and for the first time I wondered if that had been by chance or in answer to a cry for help from Nicholas.

73

Roy's mother had said that he was loyal and that, because Footfield House had been his only real home, he would always stand by the Hills. Yet that peculiar childhood, in a house where his mother had been only the housekeeper, might have led, however kind the Hills had tried to be, not to a lasting loyalty but to an incurable jealousy. The day when Roy could have turned round and thrust his own success and prosperity down their throats in a way that could never be forgiven might have been the sweetest in his life.

But it seemed that that had not happened. And that meant that besides good nature in Roy, there must be something in Nicholas to rouse affection and prevent gratitude from becoming a burden. But what had it been? Of the two, Nicholas was the more reserved, seemed to think the more slowly and to be far the less sure of himself. And did that explain it? Had he, from the start, evoked something protective in the tough little cockney?

But then, all of a sudden, I remembered that moment in the hotel when I had asked if they knew anything of Teresa Swale's having a husband, and Roy, seeming suddenly at a loss, had turned to Nicholas and Nicholas had taken over. So was the truth of it that when it came to a practical difficulty, to something which could not be solved by a quicksilver imagination and a flood of words, Nicholas was the one who took hold and said what was to be done? Was he still the dominant one, with his power so firmly established over the mind of the other that neither doubted for a moment that when Nicholas needed it, Roy would lie for him, steal if necessary, and possibly pay the bill as well?

I was not aware of it, but apparently I was frowning so hard over these thoughts that Nicholas felt impelled to break in on them and ask, "Well, don't you like it?"

Of course he knew quite well that I was not really frowning at the little town set at the mouth of a river that we were passing, or at the sea beyond it, which was turning from grey to almost the same delicate blue as the sky, with sunshine putting crests of silver onto the waves.

As I did not answer, Nicholas went on, "That breakfast's almost in sight now."

"I suppose you've often been here before," I said.

"I've visited Sheila a number of times," he said. "And I've just been doing some thinking about her. When we've assuaged your hunger, I'll ring her up from the station. . . ." He saw my expression and added, "Oh, you can listen, if you want to. I've got nothing up my sleeve. I was going to say, I'll ring her up and make sure it isn't too early for us to burst in on her, then we can go straight to her flat, you can ask your questions, find out that she, at least, doesn't know a single thing about Teresa Swale, then we can leave her in peace and find some quiet spot where we can work out a plan of campaign. Or have you got one all ready?"

"No," I said. "But I don't want to be rushed."

"Nobody's rushing you. But after talking to Sheila, you might even think the best plan would be to go back to London. The Flying Scotsman leaves at ten."

"And that isn't rushing me?"

"It's only a suggestion. You can stay in Edinburgh, of course, and do the sights. That would be educational and pleasant. I'll even take you round them. But I thought you were in a hurry to find Teresa."

"Why do you think I shan't find her here?" I asked.

"I may tell you sometime—perhaps after you've seen Sheila."

I said sharply, "I believe you know where she is all the time."

"I swear to you I don't," he said, "though by now I wish I did. But I'm ready to bet anything you like that we shan't find her in Edinburgh."

"You've a reason for saying that," I said. "You do know something."

He gave one of his rare smiles and said, "Not about Teresa, unfortunately. But keep your mind on food. Porridge. A nice kipper. Tea."

"I don't like porridge or kippers."

"They aren't compulsory."

It was a vision of a plate heaped with bacon and eggs that floated between me and my first view of the clifflike houses of grey stone that towered over the railway line as the train entered Edinburgh, and of the grey-green gulk of Arthur's Seat behind them. But it was annoying, when it presently came to the point and we sat down to breakfast in the station, that I was not nearly as hungry as I had thought and actually found difficulty in swallowing the food that I had ordered.

If only I had been alone, I thought, it would have been different, but it felt quite wrong to be sitting there eating breakfast with the husband of Teresa Swale, pouring out tea for him and then getting involved in a silly argument with him about whether or not I was to pay for myself. I made such a fuss about it that he gave in, reminding me that we were now going to telephone Sheila Hill to warn her of our coming.

Trailing around the station with him till we found a telephone box, I waited outside it while he went in, dropped pennies into the box, and started dialling, and though he propped the door open a little way so that I could listen if I wanted to, I deliberately moved out of earshot and turned my back on him.

I was standing there, waiting for him, when from about twenty yards away, staring at me across a barrow heaped with luggage, I met a pair of cavernous, dark eyes in a gaunt, white face, and for an instant I stared back, startled at the intensity of the stare, yet without recognition. But then, as the woman turned abruptly and fled and I saw the tall, angular body and the tapering velvet slacks showing under a dirty raincoat, I realised who it was and, calling out to her to wait, ran after her.

CHAPTER EIGHT

Two things prevented my catching her. One was the barrow with its pile of luggage. Just as I swerved to avoid it, a porter appeared from nowhere, gripped its handles, and pushed it right in front of me.

The other thing was Nicholas's hand on my arm.

Quietly, but in a voice that was tight with anger, he asked me where I thought I was going.

"Damn!" I said. "Oh damn! Now I've lost her."

"Lost who?"

"That woman."

"Teresa?" he said unbelievingly, but his face went white.

"No, Callie Mars. Teresa's friend. The one I told you about. And it's your fault I lost her."

He was staring across the station, but of course there was no sign of Callie now.

"I'm sorry, I thought you were running out on me," he said.

"And why shouldn't I, if I happen to want to?"

He was not a quick thinker like Roy, and it took him a moment to gesture at my suitcase, which was beside his, just outside the telephone box, and say, "You seemed to be forgetting your luggage."

"Listen," I said, doing my best to sound calm and sure of myself, "it wasn't I who had the idea we should travel together. It wasn't I who thought we should call on Mrs. Hill together. And if at any time I want to run out on you, I shall, and I don't expect to be stopped."

"If you try to run on me, you can expect to be stopped—at least until you stop messing about in the affairs of my family," he said. "Anyway, what's that woman doing here?"

"If you'd let me catch her, I might have been able to tell you."

"I suppose it's the gathering of the vultures," he said.

"Are you calling me a vulture?"

"A sort of a one, I think," he said. "Only a small one, a rather innocent one. But still, you're here to pick the flesh off the bones of the poor old corpse, aren't you? Yes, she must have been on the train, which means, I suppose, that she was following you, too. Well, let's get going. Sheila's expecting us." He picked up our two suitcases. "We'd better take a taxi."

I did not move. "Mr. Hill, you've got to understand something. I'm not here to pick the flesh off anybody's bones. Not even yours. I just want Teresa's signature on a piece of paper."

"So you keep saying."

"But you must understand . . ."

"All right, I understand," he said sharply in a tone which made it clear that he neither understood nor intended to try to do so.

"And it may have been you whom Callie's been following," I said to pay him out, following him as he strode towards the taxi-rank.

The taxi drove up the ramp onto the Waverley Bridge and turned to the left. I am not sure what I had been expecting of my first sight of Edinburgh, but I think something grey, cold, and forbidding. What I saw was not cold and forbidding at all, because there was a faint mistiness in the air, which the morning sunshine touched with iridescence and which gave the castle's great pile of stone walls and towers, which hang over the town, a curiously insubstantial look, as if they were really built out of light and shadow.

As the taxi shot off to the left and then climbed steeply, this odd illusion persisted. The cobbled street up which we went had small, dirty shops on either side and alleys leading off to right and left, in which I caught glimpses of stone steps, worn with age and rising with perilous steepness between the houses. Yet something in the angle of the light struck a gleam from the stone and made the old houses, solid as rocks, become part of a silvery pattern of light and shade.

Nicholas had his mind on something else.

"Edinburgh taxis," he said, "are damned expensive. They start at two and sixpence."

"We could have taken a bus," I said. "The taxi was your idea."

"I wasn't complaining; I was merely stating a fact," he said. "And I told Sheila we'd arrive in a few minutes. She's got to get to her job, and she hasn't got long."

"What did you tell her about me?" I asked.

"Hardly anything at all, because of your Callie Mars. I'd just got to the point of saying I'd got a girl with me, then I had to ring off."

"So she doesn't really know why we're suddenly arriving."

"No. But all the same . . ." He turned his head to give me a searching look. "You haven't been in touch with her already, have you?"

"No, I haven't."

"Yet it sounded almost as if she was expecting us. She said she knew it would be me when she heard the telephone ring."

"That sounds as if she was expecting you, not me."

"I suppose so, only she sounded extraordinarily excited. Not at all like her normal self."

"What's her normal self like?"

"Very quiet. Very reserved. You'll see for yourself. What's your plan of campaign, by the way?"

"Just to ask her if she's seen Teresa and to tell her why I want her."

"And to tell her why you think Teresa might be here."

I did not answer, and after that he asked no more questions.

A moment later the taxi took another sharp turn and stopped. We were in a short, broad street of what must once, I thought, have been handsome houses. Indeed, they were still handsome in their stark, stony way, with finely proportioned windows and stately doorways. But the whole street had the look of having come down in the world. There were one or two small shops in it, a frowzy-looking news agent, and a flyblown butcher. Rows of bulging dustbins stood along the edge of the pavement. Leaning against the area railings of the house were two girls in dirty blouses and skirts, with unkempt, frizzy hair and the remains of last night's make-up on their faces. From an open window in one of the houses opposite, a young man in his shirt sleeves, with a Teddy boy's hairdo, was shouting facetious remarks at them. There was a broken milk bottle in the gutter.

As Nicholas picked up our suitcases again and we went up the steps to the door, I thought that if Teresa Swale had come here, hoping somehow to squeeze money out of Mrs. Hill, the sight of the street in which she now lived must have been discouraging.

The heavy door stood open. Nicholas touched one of the bells beside it as he passed, then led the way up the stairs inside. They were of stone and badly worn and went up between two walls, without any kind of bannisters to hold on to. The walls looked as if no one had thought of giving them a coat of paint since before the war. We climbed and climbed.

After two or three flights, Nicholas looked round at me.

"Cheer up," he said, "this isn't actually a slum."

"What is it, then?" I asked.

"Rather a fine house, as you'll see when you've got your breath. But they've been building blocks of flats in this town since about the sixteenth century—in fact, I believe there's some claim they invented them—but unfortunately no one invented lifts till a lot later."

A door above us had opened and someone was running down the stairs towards us. On the next half landing she met us and, with a laughing cry of welcome, threw her arms round Nicholas's neck.

"Oh, Nick, this is perfect, perfect!" she cried. "But however did you know? However did manage to choose today of all days?"

There was no question about it—Sheila Hill was excited, but not in a way which could possibly have been caused by Teresa Swale.

Nicholas dumped the suitcases, returned her kiss, but extricated himself from her embrace as quickly as he could and, with a twitching together of his straight, dark brows, turned, saying, "This is Miss Purvis, Sheila, whom I was telling you about."

With a radiant smile, Sheila Hill held out a hand to me.

She was a tall, slight woman of about thirty, small-boned and delicately built and with the grace of a buoyant vitality in her movements. Her head was small and carried high on a slender neck. The hand she was holding out was narrow and fine. Her hair was of an almost silver fairness, parted in the middle, brushed back very simply from her ears, and tucked into a small knot at the back of her head. She had on a dress of light blue jersey, well-cut and close-fitting. She was not at all what I had been expecting.

The warmth of her welcome, of course, was for the girl whom she imagined Nicholas had brought to see her, all the way from London, for reasons quite unlike the real ones. But seeing in our two faces something which told her that she had gone wrong, she swept us up the remaining stairs to her flat, chattering as we went.

The flat, after the staircase, came as almost as much of a surprise as Sheila had, after Nicholas's description. It was light and spacious. The room into which she led us was lofty, with two tall windows and a carved marble fireplace. All the colours in it were clear and soft and the furniture was graceful. It was a room that suited Sheila, that was somehow like her, except in one respect, and that was that from its windows you could look straight into the room inhabited by the Teddy boy and, as I could see now, by six or seven of his younger brothers and sisters.

Sheila had gone into the room ahead of us, then had suddenly spun on her heel to face Nicholas again and, throwing out both hands in a gesture that seemed to make us free of all she possessed, exclaimed, "But I can't get over it, Nick darling, your coming just today!"

"What is it, Sheila? What's happened to you?" He smiled at her with affection, but my presence there kept him tense.

"I'm going to get married," she said. "I'm going to marry Alec. We decided yesterday, when he got back from London. He's been there for some time on business and I missed him so, so I knew . . ." She went to Nicholas and put her hands on his shoulders. "Tell me you're glad, Nick. Tell me you want it and—that you don't mind."

"Mind!" he said. "I'm delighted, Sheila. That it's Alec, too. I've thought for a long time you ought to make up your mind."

"Oh, I ought, I ought—I know that now, because I'm so happy now I have," she said. "And I thought, I felt sure, you'd be glad, but then I just wondered, because of Reggie."

Tears welled up in her eyes and she pressed her cheek against his; then she stood away from him and turned to me.

"You see why it seemed so wonderful when I heard Nick's voice on the telephone this morning, Miss Purvis," she said. "The funny thing was, as soon as the telephone rang, I felt certain it was going to be Nick. I suppose that was only because I wanted it so much, because I wanted him to be the first person I told about it. Reggie was his brother, you see, and my husband. He died seven years ago."

"Miss Purvis knows all about you," Nicholas said drily.

"And I know nothing about Miss Purvis—so why don't you tell me?" Sheila laughed as she said it, but there was a shakiness that covered tears in the sound.

I did not want Nicholas to tell her anything. I did not want to tell her anything myself. I did not want to stay. I felt more of an unwanted intruder than I had ever felt in my life, and the more friendliness I saw in her face, the worse I felt. I should have liked to grab my suitcase and turn and flee straight down that long staircase.

Nicholas saw it all in my expression and gave a sardonic smile.

"As a matter of fact, Miss Purvis takes a bit of explaining," he said. "It's quite a story; so why don't we all sit down? Then she can tell it all carefully from the beginning. And if you could find her something to eat, it might help, because she's a hungry girl. She takes quite a bit of feeding."

"Breakfast—you haven't had breakfast!" Sheila exclaimed. "What can I be thinking of?"

"We have—we had it at the station!" I said indignantly. "I'm not at all hungry. Really—please!"

She looked doubtfully at Nicholas, saw his grin, then looked back at me and said, "The trouble is, I ought to rush off. I work in a library and I ought to be there in about three minutes, which of course is impossible, but still I mustn't be too late. But you can stay here and help yourselves to anything you like. And you can have baths, if you want to. And then we could meet for lunch at one. What about that?"

It offered a respite. It meant that I could collect my wits and then possibly catch the next train back to London and let Nicholas go alone to meet her.

I was about to agree thankfully to her suggestion when Nicholas said, "Just let us ask you something before you go, Sheila. It won't keep you more than another minute or two. You see, Miss Purvis has a brother who's a journalist, and he's been writing a thing all about Teresa Swale. And just when he finished it, two things happened—he got pneumonia and had to go into hospital and Teresa herself disappeared. But, before his story can be published, her signature's needed, agreeing to its publication, so Miss Purvis is trying to find her. It was a bit of a last hope coming here, but we—we thought that just possibly you might have heard from her."

At the first mention of Teresa, all Sheila's radiance died. As if she suddenly felt very tired, she sank down onto the arm of a chair. It was not exactly hostility that I saw on her face when she spoke to me, but a sort of dreary bewilderment.

"Why should you think I might have heard from her?" she asked.

I sat down, too, and to steady my nerves, fished for a cigarette in my bag.

"I suppose because I didn't know where else to look," I said, "and I feel that I've got to do something to help my sister and her husband. They need the money for his story rather badly."

"Yes, I understand," Sheila said. "But in fact I haven't heard anything of Teresa since the trial. I wrote to her just after it, but she didn't answer. I wasn't sorry, but I'd felt I'd got to write and offer her help. She'd been through a very terrible experience."

"You believed she was innocent, didn't you?" I said.

"I didn't feel sure she was guilty," Sheila answered. "She'd no reason to kill David, not a shadow of one. And she seemed a quite goodhearted girl. It's true I'd suspected her of stealing a few little oddments of jewellery—nothing very valuable, but Reggie'd given them to me and I was worried about it. There was something about her that made one automatically distrust her honesty. I don't know what it was, except that she was always telling one how honest she was, and in a querulous sort of way, as if she didn't really expect to be believed. But there's a big difference between taking one or two brooches and doing a murder, and anyway I never had any actual evidence that she'd stolen the things. So somehow I felt better myself if I gave her the benefit of the doubt."

Again, just as I was going to speak, Nicholas got in first. "Has anyone else recently asked you if you've seen her, Sheila?"

"No one at all," she said.

"There's a woman called Mars who seems to be looking for her too; we don't quite know why," he said.

She shook her head. "I haven't seen her."

He looked at me. "Is there anything else you want to say now, Miss Purvis, or can the rest of it wait till lunch?"

"There isn't much more to say, is there?" I said.

"Then run along, Sheila," he said. "We'll see you at one. Where shall we meet?"

She sprang to her feet, her face bright again. It would have taken much more that day than the mere mention of Teresa's name to dim her happiness for long. She told us the name of a restaurant, adding, "I wish Alec were here, too, but he's gone to Hunter Law to break the news to his mother. He'll be back in Edinburgh tomorrow, so you'll see him then."

She came towards me and held out a hand.

"I'm sorry I can't help you about Teresa. Believe me, I would if I could."

"I'm sorry to have troubled you with the matter," I said.

"Don't worry about that," she said. "In your place, I hope, I'd be trying to do what you are. I'll see you and Nick later, then."

She caught up a jacket and a handbag and went running out.

I realised that I had not yet lit my cigarette and that I did not want it. Tucking it back into the packet, I went to the window and stood looking out. The boy had gone from the window opposite and it was now filled by the back of an immensely stout woman, who stood there ironing. On the steps of the house one of her younger children was sitting, carefully picking a scab off one of his knees. I saw Sheila come out and, with that light, swinging walk of hers, go quickly away down the street.

Because of the silence in the room, I said at last, "This is a queer sort of neighbourhood. A little of everything."

"Yes," Nicholas said.

After that, the silence came back.

I did not like it. I knew that I had to make up my mind, to go or to stay, but now that Sheila had gone, taking with her the tremendous pressure that she had unconsciously exerted on me to leave her happiness unclouded, I was not sure what I wanted to do. But Nicholas was waiting for me to say that I was now going to catch that train back to London.

I temporized again. "Thank you for asking my question for me. I'm not sure that I'd have been able to get it out if you hadn't."

I heard him moving across the room towards me till he stood at my side.

"Thank you for not telling her about my marriage to Teresa," he said. "But now I want to know—why didn't you?"

CHAPTER NINE

I looked hard at the broad back of the woman ironing on the other side of the street.

"I suppose because of how she looked," I said. "It would have been a pity to spoil it."

"I've never seen her look like that before," he said. "I used to see a good deal of her and I was very fond of her. But I can't remember ever having seen her look really alive before. I'm glad you didn't feel you'd got to explain to her that there's quite a possibility I arranged David's murder. All the same, it's what you believe, isn't it?"

The stout woman had waddled away from the window. She was in the inner depths of the room, a massive shadow, waving her thick arms at someone I could not see in what had the look of a noisy argument.

"It's what I'm afraid of," I said. "The trouble is, when I look at you, I can't believe it."

"I look an awful lot more like a murderer than I feel," he said. He moved away from the window and I turned and watched him as he went to the fireplace and took a long look at himself in a gilt-framed mirror that hung above it.

"I've always thought I've a rather sinister face and that I'd do quite well in the part of first or second murderer," he went on. "But I was in Rome when it actually happened, you know. You can check that if you want to."

"How?" I asked. "Detecting is an extraordinarily difficult business, when you've got ladylike scruples about asking personal questions."

"And about upsetting people when their faces are happy. Poor Elspeth, you aren't cut out for this job, are you?" he said.

"I wish I was sure that I'm cut out for any job in particular," I said, "but no doubt one just settles into something bit by bit. What were you doing in Rome?"

"I went out there in the autumn with a scholarship for a year. You can ask Roy about it, if you want to. As it happens, he was there with me at the time of the murder."

"Won't I just be told some more of the adventures of Leni Brief-bach?"

He gave a laugh. "Oh, so you've got on to Roy."

"I think I've got on to the fact that you'll back each other up through almost anything," I said.

He turned and, with his back to the mirror, stood leaning against the marble mantelshelf, watching me thoughtfully as I sat down.

"You could look at my old passport, if you like—except that it's in London," he said. "It probably shows my comings and goings. And you could ask Sheila about it. She put a trunk call through to me in Rome immediately after they found David's body, and I was there to answer it. Only the trouble is, I suppose my whereabouts doesn't signify, because you don't suspect that I did the murder myself, but that I put Teresa up to doing it. Well, where do we go from there?"

"I'm not quite sure, but I think I'm probably going back to London."

"And giving up the hunt?"

"Anyway, giving up the hunt in Edinburgh. Mrs. Hill says she hasn't seen anything of Teresa and that's really all I came to find out, isn't it? And I've never really been able to understand why Teresa should wait five years to try extorting money from Mrs. Hill by threatening to publish the story of her marriage to you—or even how Teresa could ever expect to get money from Mrs. Hill by telling her about that—because if you'd really had anything to do with the death of her child, it doesn't seem likely she'd pay to protect you. And, anyway, it doesn't look as if she's got the money to pay with."

"Exactly," Nicholas said. "Look around you. There's some nice furniture in this room, isn't there? But it's just the bits and pieces she decided not to put into the sale at Footfield House. And this flat, once you get inside, is quite grand, but it's in one of the neighbourhoods that have gone down badly, and the rent's relatively low. And she goes to work every day. It's true that's partly to keep herself sane. She could quite easily get by on what Reggie left her, just as she did at Footfield, but prices have gone up since those days and her income hasn't, so even with her salary added on, she isn't a very promising prospect for blackmail."

"On the other hand," I said, "if Teresa was desperate, even a little would come in handy."

"Yet why wait those five years until just the time when she wasn't desperate any longer—that's to say, when all she'd got to do to get a thousand pounds was to sign a piece of paper?"

"Yes, I know," I said. "But where *has* Teresa gone, then?"

I yawned enormously as I said it. I was getting very tired of Teresa. The only thing that I wholeheartedly wanted just then was to get out of the clothes that I had worn all night and to have the bath that Sheila had suggested. After that, it would be pleasant to make some coffee in her kitchen and then find a bed in the flat to lie down on and go to sleep.

"I should think there's a quite simple answer to your question," Nicholas was saying, "but it isn't dramatic. It's that she's spending a few days somewhere with some man."

I felt too sleepy to explain about the pearl earrings and the nylon blouse that Teresa hadn't taken away with her. With another helpless yawn, I said, "It's queer, you know—usually being married to

88

someone, even for a short time, seems to leave some sort of feeling behind—love, hate, sadness, contempt—something. But you talk about Teresa without any feeling at all."

"Perhaps I'm not a very feeling person," he said.

"How did you come to marry her, then? That's still another thing I can't understand. However did it happen?"

Suddenly he was angry. "I doubt very much if that's a thing I'll ever try to explain to you. Now I'm going out to get some cigarettes and a newspaper. Will you be all right here?"

He was at the door already by the time he asked the question.

I could not see why, after we had discussed his possible complicity in a murder in such a friendly fashion, my fairly innocent question should so obviously have hit a nerve.

Irritated, too, I said, "Of course I'll be all right, but suppose I run out on you."

"You're looking much too sleepy to run anywhere," he said. "I shan't be long. And if you could manage to make up your mind while I'm gone what you want to do next, it might help."

He went out and I heard the heavy old door of the flat close behind him.

I did not move at all for a minute or two after he left. But then I realised that if I did not get up and make myself do something, I should fall asleep in the chair where I was sitting. My eyelids were heavy as lead, and in the sudden quiet of the room it would have been the easiest thing in the world to go to sleep. Getting up, I went to the telephone, dialled the operator, asked for a transferred charge call, and gave the Lincolns' number.

As soon as Janet answered, I knew from her voice that she was in one of her nervous moods, though whether on Bernard's account or her own I could not tell even after I had asked her, because her nervousness, as usual, made her brusque, and she only answered snappishly that they were both all right.

Then, with her mind on the cost of a call from Edinburgh, she went on hurriedly, "Where are you, Elspeth? What are you doing?"

"I'm in Mrs. Hill's flat," I said. "I've just seen her."

"What about Teresa Swale?"

"Not a sign of her."

"Then come home, Elspeth."

"Well, I'm not sure about that," I said. "Nicholas and I are supposed to be having lunch with her and . . ."

"You and *who?*" Janet yelped.

I had forgotten that she did not know that I had had a travelling companion.

"Nicholas Hill," I said. "He came up on the same train as I did."

"Oh dear, I don't like the sound of that at all," she said. "I don't think it can have been a coincidence."

"It wasn't a coincidence," I said. "They were dogging my footsteps, those two, one covering the station and the other the airport."

"*Who* was covering the airport?"

"Roy Carney."

"When?"

"Yesterday evening," I said patiently. "Whichever way I went, one of them was to come along with me and try to put me off seeing Sheila Hill."

"Roy wasn't at the airport," Janet said. "He was here. He got here only a little while after you left and he stayed and stayed, telling me his whole history. He's had a quite amazing life. . . ." She seemed to pull herself up and, after a short pause, during which I was trying to digest what she had told me, she added, "He offered Bernard and me a thousand pounds not to publish the story of Teresa Swale."

I exclaimed something, but the sound apparently failed to reach Janet, for she went on excitedly, "Elspeth . . . Elspeth, are you there? He offered us a thousand pounds. . . ."

"Yes, I heard," I said. I understood her nervousness now. "What did you say to him?"

"Well, just to begin with, I thought how incredibly generous of him it was to offer it, simply to protect that Hill man. And at the same time it felt like the solution of all our problems. . . . Elspeth, this call is going to cost the earth."

"Never mind, go on," I said.

"You know, I was almost in tears, I was so grateful," she said. "But then I started seeing all the snags and said we couldn't possibly accept it. But after he'd gone I couldn't stop thinking about it and I didn't get to sleep all night and by now I'm in such a state of confusion, I don't know where I am. The money would be wonderful, but you see, Bernard doesn't know yet that we haven't found Teresa, or that you're in Scotland, or that we've been seeing Roy Carney, or anything. He's much better, but I haven't wanted to say anything that could start him worrying. He needs all his strength just to get back on his feet. Then there's Teresa herself. Roy didn't say if he was ready to give her a thousand pounds, too, when she turns up again, but she probably needs the money even more than we do, so it didn't seem right to contract out and leave her high and dry. And then there was something else. . . . Oh God, listen to those pips! . . . The point is, Elspeth, I've a sort of feeling that if we agreed not to publish, it'd have to be for nothing. I mean, taking money for *not* publishing almost feels like taking blackmail. Or is that stupid? I've thought about it so hard all night I can't think straight about anything any more. I feel we just could give up the idea of publishing at all, if it's really going to cause a lot of distress we didn't realise, but I don't think we could take money for doing that."

I said, "Oh Janet, we have gone and blundered into something, haven't we?"

"Yes, I know. It's all that wretched marriage, I suppose. They want to cover it up at any price. Yet of course there isn't a word about it in Bernard's manuscript and they know that."

"Roy hasn't rung you up again or anything, has he?" I asked.

"No," she said.

"Well, if he does, don't accept that money. I think that accepting anything at all from any of these people could be an awful mistake. I mean, it would sort of tie one's hands."

"I'm glad you agree with me about that," Janet said. "At least, I suppose I am. But what nightmares I've had about saying that no-thank-you! When are you coming home, Elspeth?"

"I'm not sure yet. I'm going to have a bath now and do some thinking. I'll ring up again presently, when I've decided what I'm going to do."

But I had already decided. Something about Roy Carney's offer to Janet had made me determined not to call off the search for Teresa until there was nothing more that I could do to find her. So I would at least stay till I had seen Sheila Hill again.

We said good-bye and rang off. A moment later the doorbell rang and I went to the door to let Nicholas in again.

It was not Nicholas who was standing there. It was Callie Mars.

She gave the door a sharp push, flung one long arm round me, pinioning my arms to my sides, put her other hand over my mouth, and thrust me back hard against the nearest wall.

I made one feeble attempt at struggling, but her hard, thin body was immensely strong. Behind her Lance Martin, the man whom I had seen in her room, came quietly into the flat, closed the door, and leant against it. In a swift, smooth gesture, his hand went to his breast pocket and stayed there.

"You're coming with us," Callie Mars said. "Don't make trouble and you won't get hurt. And don't think this is for fun, just because you aren't used to it. Lance hasn't any sense of fun and he's very nasty to anyone who makes trouble."

CHAPTER TEN

We went down the stairs so fast that I had hardly time to think about how dangerous I had thought them on the way up. Nothing could have seemed dangerous to me just then but the man Lance Martin, with his hand in his pocket.

If I had heard Nicholas coming up the stairs, I might have had the courage to shout, but I heard nothing at all, not a footstep, not a voice. For all I knew, the house was full of people who would have been willing to come to my help, but with its great, thick walls of stone and its heavy doors, not a sound of life reached me.

Callie's sharp-nailed fingers gripped me painfully above one elbow. Lance Martin had hold of the other. When we reached the last flight of stairs, Callie said in my ear, "Don't yell when we get to the street. Understand? Don't do it!"

I was meaning to yell, or I thought that I was. But sheer amazement, as well as fear, paralyzed me, and even if I had seen someone in the street who looked likely to want to help me, I might not have dared to shout. The feeling that my shout, however loud, would only

93

ring inside my own head, like a cry in a nightmare, dried my throat and stopped my breath.

In fact, the only people I saw in the street were the two girls who had been leaning against the area railings when I arrived with Nicholas. They were still there and did not ever turn to look as Callie and Lance rushed me across the pavement and into the car that was waiting there.

They pushed me into the back of it and Lance got in beside me. Callie drove. Lance sat with his body, which looked plump and soft, but felt as hard as a rock, pressing me into a corner of the car. I could smell the strong, sickening smell of the hair oil that made his pale hair look almost green.

As the car jerked forward, he patted my knee. "She's a good girl, Callie; she's got sense," he said.

"Then see she stays sensible—that's your job," Callie said, and swung the car sharply round the corner.

At that moment I saw Nicholas. He was coming out of a telephone box on the far side of the street. For an instant his eyes met mine and I saw his face stiffen with incredulity. Then we were past him, the car streaking along a cobbled sidestreet.

At first I thought that if Callie kept up this speed, we should be stopped by a policeman, but then I realised that she was not really driving fast. It was my own panic that made it seem as if the whole world were standing still and only we were moving.

I did not know in what direction we were going, but I thought that it was away from the centre of the city. I thought, "I'm going to yell—it isn't possible that anything can happen to me. In another moment I'm going to yell."

Then Lance patted me again with a thick, pale hand and said, "Don't worry—we're just going somewhere quiet to have a talk. Nothing for you to worry about at all."

With an effort I got my voice back. "Why can't we stop and talk here?"

"It'd be nicer to go somewhere quiet and peaceful, wouldn't it?" he said.

"For God's sake, shut up," Callie said. "I want to concentrate."

"See?" Lance said. "Her nerves keep boiling up. You don't know what I suffer from her nerves. It's best for her to go somewhere quiet."

"God damn you, my nerves are my own business!" Callie said furiously.

I shut my eyes for a moment because I was feeling dizzy and sick. I thought of Callie's voice. It had that fantastically inappropriate note of breeding, which made me think of expensive schools and Oxford. Yet at the same time it had a harshness that made it as coarse as the man's.

She was wearing the dirty raincoat and under it the same tapered velvet slacks and yellow blouse that she had been wearing when I had seen her before. The blouse was a good deal dirtier now and, sitting behind her, I had seen that her neck was dirty, too. It looked like old dirt, not just the dirt of a railway journey.

"How did you know where to find me?" I asked Lance.

"I've been keeping an eye on that place," he said. "Saw you come, saw the others go out, so it seemed like a good time to get together."

"Why were you keeping an eye on that place?" I asked.

"Well, Callie and I got thinking about Teresa's husband, see? Went to Somerset House, just like you did, only a little sooner. Saw you coming when I was leaving. Well, we found out that interesting fact about Teresa being married all this time to Hill—and never a word about it to her two best friends. A queer girl, Teresa. Always got something up her sleeve. That's the one thing I don't like about her. Well, as I was saying . . ."

"Have you got to talk such a lot?" Callie interrupted.

"I'm just politely answering what I been asked," he said. "As I was saying, Miss Purvis, when we found this out about Teresa's marriage, we thought the sensible thing was for Callie to keep an eye on young Hill and me to come to Edinburgh. We knew about Mrs. Hill being in Edinburgh, because Teresa talked about her sometimes—said she was the one person who'd been fair to her. Well, then Hill came to Edinburgh, too. Callie saw him get on the train and followed him and settled down in the next compartment. And then what does she do? She goes to sleep. That's Callie. And when she woke up, the train was in Edinburgh and Hill wasn't there. And then she saw you and him together and knew you'd recognised her, so she didn't stop to say hello, but came looking for me in the room I'd got myself opposite Mrs. Hill's flat. I was watching and I saw you and Hill arrive soon after Callie."

I thought of the Teddy boy in the room across the street and guessed that it had been from somewhere in that room that Lance had done his watching.

"But why did you come to Edinburgh? I asked. "Why have you been watching Mrs. Hill?"

"For the same reason as took you there, I shouldn't wonder," he said.

"I should be profoundly surprised," I said, "if there was the slightest similarity in our motives."

"Look, Lance," Callie said quickly, "she's the kind that starts talking in long words when she's nervous. She isn't trying to make a fool of you. Don't take any notice of her."

Lance gave a pleased-sounding chuckle, which unexpectedly developed into a roar of laughter.

"That reminds me—d'you know what they write on the litter-bins in this town?" he asked, almost beside himself with mirth. " 'The amenity of the streets is recommended to your care.' Can you believe it? 'The amenity'—God Almighty!—'is recommended . . .' " He laughed so much that he failed to get the words out the second time.

"What are you complaining about?" Callie snapped. "They write it in plain English on the other side, don't they?"

I felt a hysterical desire to join in his laughter and a violent disgust at myself because it was so hard not to. I dug my nails into my palms and ground my teeth together. If I laughed, if I could not stop laughing, I felt, I should be helplessly at his mercy.

The car turned into a busy street that seemed to be near the base of the great grey-green hump of Arthur's Seat; then a minute or two later we swung off to the left. A signpost at the corner told me that we were going to a place called Dalkeith, but I do not know whether we ever reached it, or whether we turned off before we got there. I have a vague memory of a small mining town and then of a tree-bordered road beyond, where Callie increased her speed until Lance told her angrily not to be a fool.

"D'you want to call attention to yourself?" he asked petulantly. "D'you want to get pinched?"

They wrangled with each other nearly all the time, each blaming the other for talking too much, for stupidity. It was a travesty of the sort of argument which any normally married, not very well-adjusted couple might have had towards the end of a holiday on which they had seen too much of one another.

I listened as if my life depended on it, trying to find some clue to what they meant to do with me. In the oddly domestic atmosphere, my fear lessened and I thought what a fool I had been not to call their bluff at the very start. Lance's hand in his pocket, which had seemed so sinister, had probably, as before, only been grasping a pencil. If I had shouted and fought before they got me into the car, surely they could not have done anything about it.

But from time to time panic stabbed me again, mainly because of an undercurrent of fear that I sensed in Callie. Always at a certain point in the argument, with a sudden, rather disgusting humility, she gave in, and when that happened, Lance's plump, puckered little mouth tightened in a satisfied smirk.

We left the main road presently for pleasant green lanes without any traffic and not many cottages scattered along them. Lance had moved a little away from me and now offered me a cigarette. I shook my head. He took two out of the packet, stuck them both in his mouth, lit them, then leant forward and inserted one of them in Callie's mouth.

"Slow down a bit and we can start getting down to business," he told her.

"No," she said. "I want to be in on this and I can't drive and talk."

"What else have you been doing ever since we started? Talk of talk!"

"I said *talk*," she answered. "I've got some questions of my own to ask and I'm going to ask them in my own way."

"Who's going to stop you?" he asked. "I can ask my own questions first, can't I?"

"Go on and ask them then."

"If you'll slow down . . ."

"Why the hell d'you have to keep criticizing my driving?" she said. "What's the matter with it?"

"I like to drive so's I don't get remembered by everyone I pass," he said. "That means a nice, quiet forty."

"We aren't passing anybody."

"One's always passing somebody. There's always someone to see. It's bad enough having to have you along at all, with that red hair of yours. Why couldn't you put on a hat or something?"

"The only hats I've got are things people remember," Callie said. "That's the only kind I like."

"Then you could have tied a scarf round your head, couldn't you?"

"Why didn't you say so before, if that's what you wanted?"

"Because I keep forgetting how ignorant you are. Red hair and nothing to cover it up with! Haven't you any imagination? 'Car driven dangerously by red-haired woman. . . .'" His voice was thick with contempt. "So I say, slow down!"

The car slowed so suddenly that he and I were jolted forward in our seats.

"All right, Lance," Callie said in the humble voice that worried me much more than her rasping snarl. "I'm sorry about the scarf. I should have thought."

He turned to me with a smile. "Too much education, that's what's the matter with Callie. She doesn't understand the fundamentals."

"You leave my education alone!" she almost shrieked, but she kept the car down to forty.

"She grew up a lady," he went on, ignoring her, "but, poor girl, she couldn't live up to it. I reckon it takes backbone, and where Callie's backbone ought to be, she's just got a bit of string with a few knots in it. Seems just about to hold her together and that's all."

"It takes a damned sight more backbone to go on living with you than—than . . ." Her voice died. She did not want even to mention whatever it was that she had put behind her. "Go on and ask your questions," she said, "or d'you want me to stop and go and crawl under the car? That'd hide my red hair."

"No, you just go on as you are; you're doing nicely," he answered complacently. "We'll stop somewhere up on top. There'll be a nice view from there and we can get out and stretch our legs a bit."

"Ask your questions!" she shouted. "Ask your damned questions!"

He chuckled and winked at me and I felt another stab of terror.

Yet when he went on, his voice was quite matter-of-fact, without any threat in it. He might have been some sort of civil servant with a form on a desk before him that he and I had to fill up between us before I could obtain some amenity of the Welfare State.

"Well, first, Miss Purvis," he said, "I'd just like to know your real reason for wanting to find Teresa. You told her landlady and you told Callie you came from a lawyer's and you'd got some papers for her to sign so's she could get some money. Now Callie and me don't believe that any more. In fact, I may say I never believed it. So first I want to know why you really want Teresa."

"I don't mind answering that," I said, "but first there's a question I'd like to ask you."

"Ask away," he said generously.

"Why do you want to find Teresa?"

"You see," Callie said viciously, "it isn't going to be so easy, asking your questions."

Suddenly and violently he swore at her and I saw her thin shoulders writhe as if the words had been blows.

Turning back to me, he was the civil servant once more. "We're afraid she may have come to some harm, Miss Purvis. You can understand that, can't you?"

"I'm not sure that I can," I said. "Why are you afraid of that?"

"Because of her going off like that without saying anything to anyone. That's not like her. We're very old friends; we know her ways. It's not like her to go away without saying something to Callie."

That was not what I had gathered when I first saw Callie Mars, but it seemed pointless to say so.

"My reason for wanting her is rather a complicated one," I said. "That's why I made up the story about coming from a lawyer and having papers for her to sign. It seemed a simpler thing to tell you than the truth, which is that my brother-in-law, who's a journalist, has written a story all about her, and it's going to appear in *Alarum* under her name—I mean, as if she'd written it herself. And *Alarum's* paying her a thousand pounds for it and my brother-in-law a thousand, but they won't pay until she's signed a statement that she agrees to the publication. And my brother-in-law's in hospital with pneumonia, so he can't trace her himself, and that's where I come in. I'm trying to find her for him."

Callie gave a shrill cackle of laughter. My answer seemed to strike her as immeasurably funny. But Lance's pudgy face turned ugly.

"A thousand pounds—Teresa had a thousand pounds coming to her?" he said. "This is the truth?"

Callie laughed wildly again. "Holding out on us, wasn't she, Lance? You never knew anything about that thousand pounds. When we said the other day we'd like a little back of what she owes me, she told us she'd got money coming to her from her husband's family and we just didn't believe it. One of Teresa's dreams of grandeur, you said. So she's slipped through your fingers, she and her thousand pounds."

"Now wait," he said in a flat, calm voice. "Just wait while I think. This isn't as simple as it sounds."

"Good old Sherlock," she said. "If you listen carefully, Miss Purvis, you'll hear his brain ticking."

He kneaded his knuckles together and chewed his thick little lower lip, making a great effort to ignore her.

"It doesn't make sense," he said decisively after a moment. "No,

I don't think you're telling the truth, Miss Purvis. Suppose you try again.

I had been growing almost confident during the last few minutes, but now panic invaded me again.

"It *is* the truth," I said. "What doesn't make sense about it?"

"If Teresa'd had a thousand pounds coming to her, she wouldn't have cleared off."

"I know, that's what you'd think. But she did."

"Why?"

"I don't know."

"You know quite a lot."

"Not about why she went away or where she went to."

"Try again," he said. "We haven't got all day."

"But it *is* the truth," I said helplessly, and would have started to tell him the story all over again if, with a movement so fast that I had no inkling that it was coming, he had not suddenly stamped on one of my feet.

I screamed with the shock and the pain.

In a businesslike voice, Callie said, "If there's going to be any of that, I'm going to stop the car."

"Keep driving!" he shouted. As the car jolted forward again, he added, "Perhaps there won't have to be any more of that. Now, Miss Purvis, take your time, but then I want the truth."

I was blinded by tears and was shaking all over. I thought that he must have broken all the bones in my foot. I thought desperately, then blurted out, "Well then, I think it's something to do with Leni Briefbach, but I don't know what. If I only knew, I shouldn't have to be trailing around looking for Teresa."

"Who's this Leni Whatever-you-said?" he demanded.

"I don't *know!*" I wailed. "She's someone Roy Carney knew when he was in Intelligence. He—he said something about her that I didn't really understand. And he's looking for Teresa, too, you know—or don't you? He came back to England on purpose to find her."

"And she's hiding from him, is that what you mean?"

"It looks like it, doesn't it?"

"But this Leni woman—where does she come in?"

"I don't know. I rather think she's dead. I think she was executed at the end of the war. But I think Teresa must know something about her that Roy Carney wants to find out."

"And this story about your brother-in-law and *Alarum?*"

"It's all perfectly true, but there has to be a reason why Teresa ran away just when she was expecting money, and the only reason I can think of is that she was frightened."

"Why did you think she might have come to Edinburgh? It was something to do with Fenwick, wasn't it?"

"Fenwick?" I said in bewilderment.

"Alexander Fenwick," Lance said. "The Hill woman's lover. He's got money. He's the only one in that lot that's got any money."

"Oh," I said.

"Big money," Lance said. "He's Fenwick's Whisky. And I suppose there's a kind of sense in it, if you put it all together. Teresa's got this money coming to her from the papers, but then this Carney turns up and he's got something on her so she runs out, and she runs to where there's money and where she's got some pull. Still, I don't get why she's kept clear of the Hills all this time. The young chap's her husband, isn't he? Callie and me looked that up at Somerset House, first like you did. And even if he's not loaded, the odd twenty pounds from time to time would have made quite a difference to Teresa. And it's he who'd have run into trouble if she'd started to talk, not Teresa. She'd been acquitted of the murder of that kid; she was all right. But she could have made things hot for him."

"Perhaps she did," Callie said.

"Eh?" he said. "What d'you mean?"

"Perhaps she did and perhaps she's been drawing a nice little pension from him all this time and hiding it away in a sock," Callie said. "She held out on you about the thousand pounds, so why not about a little pension?"

"By God, if that's what she's been doing . . . !"

Speaking maliciously, as if she felt that she had scored, Callie said, "You see, Miss Purvis, as I told you, I lent Teresa some money. Not anything like a thousand pounds, of course. But she's got so much to be grateful to Lance for—I mean, his fatherly interest and only taking such a reasonable percentage of her earnings. So naturally he feels she owes him a good deal of that thousand, particularly as he knows a few things about her. That's always worth more than an IOU."

"Shut your mouth," he growled. "It isn't that thousand I'm after. If Teresa's cleared out when that money's coming, it's because she's got her eye on something bigger. That's how I figure it. And that's what she's going to cut us in on."

In disgust I said, "Perhaps you figure it all wrong, Mr. Martin. Perhaps Teresa never came to Edinburgh at all."

"She came," he said. "She came, but maybe she didn't stay. Maybe she's gone to see Fenwick."

"That's not what I think," Callie said. She let the car slow down. "Any objection if we stop for a bit so that I can put that question of my own that I want to ask?"

"No, all right," he grunted.

We had left the green lanes behind by then and had climbed up on to a high shoulder of moorland. Dipping and rising, the road wound on ahead, a grey streak across the dun-coloured hills. It was too early for the heather to be out, and where it grew it showed only as irregular patches of brown. Here and there bracken made a splash of emerald and willow herb a rosy cloud against the hillside. I had long ago lost all sense of direction. The names of the villages on the signposts that we had passed meant nothing to me, and I had no idea where I was.

Callie drove the car off the road onto the turf beside it, then turned, hooked an elbow over the back of it and, fixing her cavernous eyes on my face, said, "Look, this is what I want to know—what have they done with the body?"

I ought to have known at once what she meant. But the image evoked in my mind by her words was that of a child's body, spread-

103

eagled on a paved path under a high window. That body was probably in a green churchyard in Gloucestershire.

Staring dizzily back at Callie, I said, "If only I could understand the *reason* for the murder. . . ."

She twisted farther round in her seat.

"So murder *is* the answer!" she cried triumphantly. "You see, Lance. Who's right now? I don't believe a word about Teresa running out because she was afraid of something. That girl always thought she could get away with anything. If she cleared out when she ought to have been around to sign that paper, it was because she didn't know there was a paper to be signed and thought she could get the thousand pounds from *Alarum* and a lot more from Fenwick. And the Hills did her in before she could get at him, or else he did it himself, to cover up for them. And if only you can find the body before the police do, you'll be on to the best thing in your life."

I had pulled myself together a little. "I swear to you I don't know a thing about where Teresa is, alive or dead," I said. "It was the murder of David Hill I meant."

"For the Lord's sake, why drag that up now?" Callie said impatiently. "The question is, which of them killed her—Hill, the woman, or Fenwick? Or is that man Carney in on it, too? Did they get him back from America to do their killing for them?"

"I don't know," I said.

"Where did they kill her?"

"I don't know."

"Up here or in London?"

My voice rose. "I don't know! Can't you understand—I'm here simply to try to find her? I never met any of these people until two or three days ago. I'm not in with them on any murder. And I didn't come here to blackmail any of them with anything I've found out either. I haven't found anything out."

She gave a sigh and slumped back in her seat. "You sound as if you're speaking the truth—in which case, we've been wasting time and trouble. My own idea is, Teresa never came here at all. I wish I hadn't troubled to follow Hill all the way here."

"You never want to go anywhere at all," he said. "You just want to stay in that dump of yours and water your blasted plants."

"And what's wrong with that?" she demanded. "As it happens, I'd like to get back to them before they're all ruined by that Popski. I don't trust him to look after them properly."

"If they die, you can buy some more," he said.

"You don't understand," Callie said passionately. "What I can't bear is *failing* with a plant. If you start to do a thing at all, you should do it properly. You shouldn't start a thing and then go rushing off after something else. You should stick to it. You should work at it. I didn't like handing over all the responsibility to Popski."

Lance gave a nasty laugh. "Listen to the great success."

"I *am* a success with my plants!"

"Go back to your damned plants then, but I'm not through here yet," he said. "I've started a thing and, as it happens, I'm going to stick to it; I'm going to work at it." He grasped the handle of the door nearest to him and looked at me. "Come on out," he said. "This is as far as we're taking you."

I felt amazed relief. To be alone on the empty moorland, instead of in that car, seemed so wonderful a prospect, so sane, so safe, that I could hardly believe that it was actually being offered to me.

I moved my foot with care. It hurt, but less than I expected.

"Come on, come on," Lance said, holding the door open for me. "Don't take all day about it. You aren't injured for life. I'm sorry we can't take you back to town, but we'd sooner drop you off where there's no one to hear you yelling before we're out of sight. You'll appreciate that, I'm sure, and you'll be able to thumb a lift quite soon, I expect."

I did not worry at all about the lift. I thought the quiet slopes of grass and bracken, the glittering stream in the valley, and the blue of the more distant hills the friendliest sight that I had ever seen. Slithering along the seat of the car, I put my uninjured foot down on the turf, stood on it, then tested my weight on my other foot.

That made the pain worse. Walking, I thought, would be a problem. In fact, I should simply have to sit by the roadside until a car came by. From the amount of traffic that we had seen, that might mean waiting for half an hour or so, and perhaps the first car would not stop for me. But what of it? Callie and Lance would not be there. I hobbled a few steps forward.

When something came crashing down on the back of my head, I felt only one pang of unbelievable agony, then was lost in darkness.

CHAPTER ELEVEN

When the darkness cleared, there seemed to be nothing in the world but greyness and cold. The cold was all through me and the greyness all over me.

Opening my eyes, shutting them, making an effort and opening them again, I saw what looked like a grey blanket stretching in all directions. After a moment, I discovered that I was lying flat on my back, staring straight upward. The blanket was merely the sky, hidden in clouds and rain. I was lying on some soggy grass and I was wet through.

It took me some time to make up my mind to try to move. I was not in pain, but I was afraid that if I moved I should discover that I had been horribly injured. Perhaps my skull had been cracked. Perhaps my back had been broken. My memory of the scene by the road-side was still hazy, but the faces of Callie Mars and Lance Martin swam before me.

At last I found the courage to sit up. It was quite easy, but I immediately wanted to be sick.

When I had got that over, I felt a little better, though I had started a convulsive shivering. The back of my head, I found, was very tender, and the foot on which Lance had stamped, with what I thought must have been steel-shod shoes, was swollen and sore. The skin on my instep had been broken and bled a little through my stocking. One shoe was missing. But apart from that, there seemed to be nothing serious the matter.

I realised that I could not stay where I was, but to stand up was a good deal more difficult than to sit up. As soon as I tried, everything swam round me and blackness started to close in from the edges of my mind. I bent my head forward, then after a moment raised it again and looked round.

I was in a marshy hollow, where reeds grew almost as thickly as grass and the ground was as sodden as the rain-filled air. To begin with, it puzzled me how I had got there; then I decided that Lance and Callie must have carried me to where I should be out of sight of the road, so that they would have plenty of time for their getaway.

I did not think it likely that they had carried me far. If I climbed upwards, I thought, I should probably find the road at the top of the hill. The slope was not very steep and was mainly covered with heather, crisscrossed with winding sheep tracks. Here and there the hillside was dotted with stolid, black-faced sheep. One of these looked round with faint interest in my movements, then went back to munching grass.

When the dizziness had passed, I got to my feet. Moving brought on various minor pains, but at least it helped to counteract the shivering. After I had gone a few steps, I began to retain confidence and thought that it would not be too difficult to reach the hilltop. If I had had both shoes, instead of only one, I should have reached it in a few minutes, but stepping with my stocking-covered sole on sharp twigs of heather was painful and made my progress slow. I was dreadfully assailed by the temptation of tears, feeling with the blind certainty that one does at such times that if I simply sat down and cried, someone was sure to come to my rescue.

Then at last I was through the heather and out on hummocky

grass. I limped the rest of the way to the top of the hill fairly quickly, and there, as I had expected, I found the road stretching away to right and left into the curtain of the rain. After only a few minutes, I heard a car coming. It was small and old and the sound of it coming at a staid thirty miles an hour was one of the pleasantest things that I have ever heard in my life.

Waving a thumb frantically, I felt hopeful until the car was almost abreast of me; then I was in despair, because I knew that it would pass. It did pass, but after it had gone only a few yards beyond me, it stopped, backed, and the door was opened.

"You'll be wanting a lift," the driver stated quietly.

He was a thin old man, with a weather-beaten face and grey hair.

I could not have answered if I had tried. I did not try. Limping forward, I scrambled into the car and pulled the door shut. Then the shivering started again and, as the car started forward, I dropped my head into my hands and found that this time I could not stop the tears.

The driver did not remark on this, and for some distance he and I did not exchange a word.

This surprised me, because I knew what I must look like, and I had been expecting a string of questions. When at last he spoke, I had no impulse to dispute what he said.

"The weather," he said, "is very inclement."

"Oh, it is," I said, thankful to find that my voice was under control. "That's just what it is."

"I'm going to Duns myself," he said. "I'm not acquainted with your destination."

"I don't much mind where I go to," I said, "if I can get to Edinburgh in the end."

"Och, that's in the opposite direction," he said with concern. "But this is no weather for you to be standing out by the roadside, and I'm thinking you're in no shape for doing it either."

"Never mind, just take me to wherever you're going yourself," I said. "If I got out and waited for a car going the other way, there's no telling how long it might be before someone would stop for me."

"Ay, that's very hypothetical," he agreed gravely.

"You're very kind indeed to give me the lift—I'm very grateful," I said.

"You're very welcome," he said.

"So if you'll just drop me anywhere I can find a telephone, I'll be all right."

He nodded and said, "I'll just be turning over in my mind what's best to be done. I see you've lost your shoe and your purse. Lassie, if I'd a daughter your age, I'd not allow her out on the road, hitchhiking from place to place, but I'm aware you'll not be much interested in my opinion."

And that was the nearest he came to making any direct reference to my predicament.

His words had started a new worry in my mind. Until he spoke, I had entirely forgotten that my handbag, with all my money in it, was still in Sheila's flat. And, even to telephone, I should need money. It began to look as if the only thing for me to do was to ask this kind old man to drive me to a police station. Long ago I had been carefully instructed that this was the correct thing to do if ever I was stranded in a strange place without money.

Yet I felt an extreme reluctance to do it. In a police station, I thought, I should be given cups of tea, which would be pleasant, and asked questions, which at the moment would be distressing. For one question would lead to another, and before I knew where I was, I should be talking about Teresa Swale and murder; and what was a stolid Scottish constable, here in the middle of nowhere, going to make of that?

Only, of course, we weren't in the middle of nowhere. We couldn't be.

"How far are we from Edinburgh?" I asked.

"Twenty-five–thirty miles," the old man said.

"Is that really all?" My nervous system rejected the information. The experiences of the last few hours, together with the empty expanse of the moor, shrouded in rain, made me feel as if we might be fifty miles from the nearest dwelling.

"Ay, it's not a great way," he said. "We're on the Lammermuirs the now. You're from the South?"

"Yes, from London."

"I was in London once," he said. "A long time back—1914. A grand city, but it'll have changed since then, I don't doubt. You've friends in Edinburgh?"

I was not sure if I could call the Hills friends, but I nodded.

"We'll give them a call then at the first telephone we come to, and if they're not at home, we'll think again. I'm thinking you shouldn't stay in those wet clothes any longer than need be."

"I'm all right," I said. "You mustn't worry about me. You're being awfully kind."

"We'll be passing the New Inn in a few minutes," he said. "We'll stop there and use their telephone."

I noticed that he had taken it on himself to make the call, and I knew that this was because of the absence of my handbag. I wanted to thank him, but when I tried to start, I felt that I was going to burst into tears again. I doubt if I have ever felt such an intensity of gratitude as I did to this kind, incurious man, but it was beyond me to tell him so.

"Yon's the inn," he said after a moment, "and if you won't be offended at the suggestion, I'm thinking that a wee dram wouldn't do you any harm. It'll help to keep the cold out."

I said that I thought it would be wonderful, and this time I managed to thank him, at least for the whisky, though not for all the reassurance that he was giving me.

We had been going downhill for the last few minutes and the New Inn was below us, a small, whitewashed building beside a stream. Opposite the inn, the road forked and a white signpost stood at the corner, with arms that pointed along the two narrow roads ahead, telling us that both of the roads led to Duns and to Berwick.

There were several other names on each arm which were not the same, and on one I saw, as we got out of the car and I limped after him into the inn, a name that seemed familiar. I paused to make sure of it and read, "Hunter Law—3½ miles."

In the inn the old man ordered the whisky, then asked me for the name of my friends, hunted it up in a directory, talked to the exchange, dropped coins into the box, and, only when he heard the telephone start to ring in Sheila's flat, handed the instrument over to me and went away, leaving me to speak to her in private.

But the telephone only went on ringing, unanswered.

By the time that he returned, I had hung up and was finishing my whisky.

"There's nobody at home," I said, "so I'm not sure what I ought to do next, but I've had an idea. Which of these roads to Duns is the one you take?"

"It's immaterial," he answered.

"Would it take you out of your way to go by Hunter Law?"

"It's not out of my way at all."

"Well, there's someone there who—who's a friend of my friends. If you dropped me there, I could stop bothering you."

"It's no bother, and if you're sure it's what you want to do, it's a solution, seemingly," he said. "Are you sure, though, lassie? I'll willingly take you to Duns and put you on the bus there for Edinburgh, but it's your wet clothes I'm thinking about and how you'll manage without your shoe."

"Yes, I'm quite sure," I said.

"Then we'll go by Hunter Law. What's the name of your friend's friend?"

"Fenwick," I said. "Alexander Fenwick."

"If that's who it is, you'll be well taken care of," he said. "Come away, then."

We went out into the rain again, got into the car, and drove off.

The road now wound round the foot of a hill, with birches and rowans on either side; then presently there were hedges, too. The moors were left behind us and woods, green fields, and cottages began to appear.

We had also left the rain behind by the time that we reached Hunter Law. The pale sky was flecked with only a few puffs of cloud, and sunshine made the green of the meadows brilliant.

Hunter Law was a hamlet at a crossroads, with a few bigger houses dotted around it, a church, and a manse. The Fenwicks' house, to which my friend did not need to ask the way, was some distance beyond the crossroads, a Georgian house, half hidden from the road by trees. The gates at the bottom of the short drive were open.

Driving straight in, we stopped in front of the pillared portico.

"Are you sure you'll be all right now?" the old man asked as I opened the door of the car. "I'll not intrude on your friends, but I can wait a wee while at the bottom of the drive, and if there's no one at home, you can wave; then I'll pick you up and take you on to Duns."

"I'm certain I'll be all right," I said. "And I don't know how to thank you. You've been so—so very——"

What I wanted to thank him for was the feeling of safety that there had been in that little car, chugging through the rain, after the horror that there had been in the other that had taken me up onto the moorland. But how could I find words to say that?

"So very kind," I said lamely, holding out my hand to him.

He shook it, gave me a smile, and drove off. I stood watching until he reached the end of the drive; then I limped up the steps to the door.

It was wide open. Inside I saw a paved hall, several tall doorways, and a soaring staircase, with bannisters of wrought iron. And, facing me at the other end of the hall, I saw my own image in a gilt-framed mirror. The sight so shocked me that it took me a moment to make up my mind to ring the bell.

As if that diffident touch had released a mechanism, one of the doors before me swung open and a woman came out. She was about seventy years old, was short and very broad, and was dressed in a loudly checked tweed which made her look even shorter and broader than she was. She had a big, pink, square face, pale blue eyes, and white hair. Trotting towards me down the hall with the look of relentless purpose of someone starting a cross-country race, she came straight up to me and started feeling my sleeves and my sides with thick-fingered, muscular hands.

"Why, you're soaked, my dear, absolutely soaked," she said. "Whatever have you been doing to yourself? You must have met with an accident."

I reared nervously away from her touch.

"Are you Mrs. Fenwick?" I asked. "I'm sorry to trouble you like this, but——"

She interrupted, "Of course I'm Mrs. Fenwick. Who are you?"

I started to tell her my name and that I knew Sheila and Nicholas, but she interrupted again, "Well, that can wait. You'd better get out of those wet clothes and into a hot bath just as fast as you can."

She slipped an arm through mine and drew me towards the staircase.

I was too dazed and exhausted to protest any more. Only asking her if she would telephone Nicholas to tell him where I was, I let her take me to the bathroom and help me peel off my wet clothes while hot water gushed out of the tap into the huge old bath. It looked as if it was at least fifty years old, but it was in a room that made it look like a startling piece of modernity. The walls were panelled, the ceiling was a mass of moulded plaster flowers and cherubs, and the wide, dark floorboards had the polish of centuries. A tall sash window looked out over a terrace and rose garden enclosed by stone walls. A peacock strolled languidly along the terrace.

When I stepped into the bath, Mrs. Fenwick left me, taking all my clothes with her, and a moment later she returned with a pair of striped pyjamas, a purple velvet dressing gown, and some gold mesh bedroom slippers. Then she left me again, still moving at her slow, cross-country trot, and I lay back, sinking into the hot water, hair and all, in a state of fuddled relief and bewildered thankfulness. Before I knew what was happening to me, my eyelids began to droop and odd things to crowd together in my mind with the apparent normality that governs a dream at the time of dreaming.

But I knew that somehow my smarting eyes had to be kept open. Rubbing them helped a little. But then, as I gazed upwards, I saw a large, naked, white child start to fall slowly towards me from somewhere far above. I saw it falling, falling. In another moment it was going to crash on the terrace. . . .

I sat bolt upright in the bath, panting. The child was only one of the plaster cherubs in the ceiling. All the same, I did not like the way it was looking at me, seeming to be laughing at me because it knew certain things that I did not. Or did I know them? Was that why the fat-faced creature was laughing? It seemed to me that after all I did know certain things, but that they would not come together except in a preposterous dream form and that the only way ever to make sense of them would be to let the dream spread its dark nonsense over my consciousness.

That would not do. I made another effort, washed quickly, and got out of the bath.

The pyjamas were a man's and too long in the leg for me. The dressing gown was obviously Mrs. Fenwick's and was a good deal too wide and too short. Only the gold slippers fitted me. When I was dressed, I was a curious-looking object, but I felt warm and comfortable. I was trying to comb my wet hair into some sort of shape when Mrs. Fenwick returned.

"Tea, now," she said cheerfully. "I don't know if you're hungry, but I've told them to boil you a couple of eggs, just in case. And your room'll be ready in a few minutes, so you can go to bed if you like. And I've spoken to Sheila on the telephone and she's doing her best to find Nicholas, to tell him you've arrived safely. But it appears he's been going round in circles all day, nearly out of his mind, so where he's got to by now nobody seems to know exactly."

"But I can't possibly stay here, Mrs. Fenwick!" I exclaimed. "I mean, I can't just walk in, have a bath, and go to bed, as if—as if I were someone you know."

"I'd like to know what else you can do," she said.

"If you'd just dry my clothes and tell me about the busses to Edinburgh——"

"And not hear what this is about?" She turned to the door. "My dear, you're in no position to argue. Now come along and have tea.

You needn't worry about how you look—there's no one here but me at the moment. We'll have tea and you can tell me how you got here."

"It was really just an accident," I said as I followed her out into the passage, "or a whole lot of accidents."

"I don't believe in accidents," she said as she started to descend the long, graceful staircase. "Everything's part of a plan. That's something I've been trying to prove to Nick for a long time, you know, because he's psychic and it's a terrible thing to waste any gifts you possess, and that's just what the stubborn creature's doing, even after all I've said to him. He foretold the death of that poor child, you know."

"He *what?*" I said.

"Oh yes," she said. "When Sheila wrote to him, telling him she'd engaged a nurse called . . ." She stopped and looked back at me. "There, that's just like me—no memory at all for names or faces."

"Teresa Swale," I said.

"Teresa Swale—that's right. Imagine your knowing that! Well, when Sheila wrote to him about that, Nick wrote back a frantic letter, telling her to get rid of the woman at once, or he was sure there'd be trouble. And yet he'd never seen her in his life. He swore solemnly to Sheila that he hadn't. And when he and the woman met, he didn't even recognise her."

"Did she recognise him?" I asked.

"Well, of course she'd seen his photograph in the house," she said, "so that was different."

She jogged on downstairs, across the hall, and through a door that was standing open.

I was following, but halfway down the stairs I had to pause again, to roll up the bottoms of the pyjamas that I had on, because they were entangling themselves with the golden slippers.

When I stood up, I saw a man standing in the portico, staring up at me.

I knew at once that I had seen the stocky, tweed-clad figure before. For a moment I could not have said when or where, and I did not like the feeling. For the sense of recognition was so strong that it made it seem as if what Mrs. Fenwick had said must be true and that there had been nothing accidental about my coming here—that I must have come here simply to meet this man whom I did not know.

But as I went on down the stairs, I suddenly remembered where I had seen him. He was the man whom I had seen, two evenings before, come out of the garden of Footfield House and go along the road to Mrs. Bullock's cottage.

117

CHAPTER TWELVE

With that recollection, the sense of something sinister in our meeting faded. He was not really a sinister-looking man. He had a square, blunt-featured face, very like Mrs. Fenwick's, except that the eyes were dark and calm, without the gleam of rather wild enthusiasm that sparkled in hers. His smile, as he recognised the various garments I was wearing, was one of friendly irony.

"I think you more or less answer to the description I've been given of a young woman called Elspeth Purvis," he said. "I'm glad you got here safely."

At the sound of his voice, Mrs. Fenwick came jogging back into the hall.

"Oh Alec, you're back. Then you can ring up Sergeant Stuart for me and tell him we've got Miss Purvis here," she said. "I've already rung up Sheila, and she's going to pass the news on to Nicholas. And now Miss Purvis is going to tell us all about how she got here, because she says Nicholas can't really have known she was coming, as she didn't know that herself until she was practically here. So it's plainly another case of Nicholas's peculiar powers. And this time I'm going to make him admit it." She thrust a strong arm through mine. "Now come and have tea."

"Is Sergeant Stuart the police?" I asked as we went towards the drawing room.

"Yes, of course," she said. "Nicholas has spent the day alerting most of the police in the country and in between whiles ringing up here to ask if you'd arrived yet. Of course, he's very excitable, as these people with abnormal sensitivity so often are. They carry a far greater burden than most of us, particularly when they don't understand their own powers. But we're going to put that straight between us."

"Only I don't really think this is a case of abnormal sensitivity," I said. "I'm afraid it's just that he thinks he knows how my mind works. I mean, he thinks he knows a reason why I might have come here even without—without the accident that happened."

"Ah, I want to hear all about that accident," she said. "But have some tea first. And your eggs. Lightly boiled—I hope you like them lightly boiled."

Alec Fenwick had followed us into the drawing room.

"Mother puts the creature comforts even before second sight," he said. "That accident—just what kind of accident was it?"

I did not want to talk about it. I was thinking of my glimpse of him at Footfield and wondering if it had been true that he was the new owner of Footfield House. Avoiding his eyes, I looked round the room. It was big and beautiful, with panelled walls and tall windows opening on to the terrace that I had seen from upstairs. The peacock that I had seen then was strolling regally by, swaying its tail with the dignity of an Edwardian beauty, managing the long train of a ball dress.

"What a wonderful creature that peacock is!" I exclaimed. "I didn't know you could keep them as far north as this."

"No difficulty about that at all," Mrs. Fenwick said, sitting down behind the loaded tea table, close to the wood fire that burned in the marble fireplace. "It isn't the climate they mind; it's the foxes. Now

Alec, please do go and telephone Sergeant Stuart that he can call off the hunt for Miss Purvis."

As her son nodded and went out, she went on, "Yes, foxes are the enemy. I've sometimes speculated about the feelings of an inexperienced Scottish fox, picking up a nice bird scent, then suddenly finding himself face to face with an exotic thing like that. You'd think it would be quite a shock. But perhaps a fox hasn't much of an eye for distinctions, and peacocks, geese, and turkeys are all one to him. Sugar, Miss Purvis?"

We went on chatting about the peacock until Alec returned.

I should have liked to have gone on with it after that, putting off the moment of explaining myself, but as he sat down, reaching for the cup of tea that his mother had poured out for him, he said, "Now let's hear about the accident." If there was a trace of amusement in his voice, there was also the quiet firmness of someone who is used to having his orders carried out.

I started on one of my boiled eggs. The trouble was that, without mentioning Nicholas's marriage, I could not explain why Teresa's remark that she was going to get some money from her husband's family should have got me into the clutches of Callie and Lance and then led me to Hunter Law. Yet, as I had been confusedly working out during the past hour, and as Nicholas himself had obviously worked out far more quickly than I had, Hunter Law was the logical place to expect to find Teresa. For Alec Fenwick was rich, a fact that Nicholas had carefully refrained from mentioning to me. And that must have been because he had realised that as soon as I knew it, I should have guessed that Alec was Teresa's real quarry. His wealth seemed to be the answer to that question about her actions that had so puzzled me—the question of why she had let the sleeping dogs lie for five whole years before trying to get money from her husband's family. She had merely waited, it appeared, until Sheila had made up her mind to marry Alec Fenwick.

"Well?" he said quietly.

"Mr. Fenwick, before I tell you about that, there's something else I want to tell you," I said. "It's that I've seen you before. It was on

120

Thursday evening, in Footfield. I saw you come out of Footfield House."

His mother exclaimed in astonishment.

"Well?" Alec Fenwick said again.

"Is it true that you're the new owner?" I asked.

"Yes," he said.

"Why, Alec!" his mother said. "Does Sheila know that?"

"No," he said. "Now let's get back to that accident."

Without stopping to think any more, I blurted out another question. "Mr. Fenwick, have you seen Teresa Swale?"

He showed no surprise. "You mean recently, don't you?"

"Yes," I said. "During the last few days."

"The answer is no, I'm afraid. Was she somehow involved in this accident of yours?"

"No, but some friends of hers were," I said. "A woman called Callie Mars and a man called Lance Martin. They got me into their car and drove me up on to the Lammermuirs; then they dumped me there and drove away."

"Inflicting a certain amount of damage in the process, from the look of things," he said.

"Well, yes," I said.

"And just why did they behave so unkindly?"

I answered frigidly, "It wasn't at all funny, Mr. Fenwick. They banged me on the head and dumped me in a swamp and left me. And if it hadn't been for a very kind man in an Austin Seven, I might be there still."

"I know—Archie Grant," he said. "I met him. He was worried about you. But just why did these disagreeable people treat you like that? They must have had a reason."

"They thought I knew the whereabouts of Teresa Swale," I said.

"And do you?"

"I'm looking for her myself," I said.

He nodded. "That's what Sheila told me. Nick saw you in the car, you know. He thought from your face you mightn't be there entirely of your own free will, and then he returned to Sheila's flat and found your handbag there. He concluded that meant that you'd been taken forcibly away, and he telephoned the police and they've been on the look out for you and for a red-haired woman who was driving the car and for a man of undistinguished appearance. And I've just telephoned our Sergeant Stuart that you've been found, and he's on his way round to ask you to make a statement. I thought I'd just tell you that to prepare you. It's possible you may not want to mention Teresa Swale and that you might, on consideration, prefer to let him gather that you merely accepted a lift from those two friends of hers."

"For heaven's sake, Alec," Mrs. Fenwick exclaimed, "what a thing to suggest to the poor child! If I were in her place, I'd be yelling blue murder against the pair of them."

"But you aren't in her place, my dear," he said. "You don't happen to be interested in Teresa Swale."

"But I am," she said sharply. "I'm intensely interested in the way her name keeps cropping up. Only a few minutes ago I found myself talking about her. Quite suddenly, for no particular reason. It wasn't Miss Purvis who put her into my mind. And I didn't pay any particular attention to it at the time, although I don't suppose I've given the woman a thought for years. And now you're talking about her, too, which I don't think you've done for years either. It's just as if she's *forcing* her way into our conversation, whether we like it or not."

"If it's only our conversation she forces her way into, we needn't worry," Alec said. "But there's a simple enough reason why she's on your mind today, mother. It's because you heard yesterday that Sheila and I are going to get married at last; so your thoughts have been going back to that old, sad business at Footfield."

"Perhaps—and perhaps there's more to it than that," Mrs. Fenwick said darkly.

Her son gave me a smiling look.

"My mother lives half in and half out of the world that most of us make do with," he said. "On a more terrestrial level than she can accustom herself to. It seems to me that the reason we're all of a sudden talking about Teresa Swale so much is that you've turned up, Miss Purvis. But I hope it will be possible to leave her out of your statement to the police." As he said it, it sounded like more than a hope. It sounded like a demand and one to which he was certain that I would agree.

"Did Mrs. Hill tell you why I'm looking for her?" I asked.

"She did," he said. "I hope it's the real reason."

I put down my teacup. I started to stand up. "If you're doubtful of my motives——"

He laid a hand on my shoulder and pushed me down into my chair again.

"However doubtful I am, you can't go anywhere in my mother's dressing gown, can you?" he said. "And in the middle of tea, too. No, Miss Purvis, I'm really not hinting dark things against you. In a way, I'm rather grateful to you for having made us all start thinking and talking about Teresa Swale. She's been tabu for a long time. And it might be best, after all, when Sheila and I are making a new start in our lives, to make up our minds about what we believe really happened at Footfield. But as I mentioned a minute or two ago, Sergeant Stuart is on his way here, and it seems to me, if your reason for wanting Teresa is just what you've told us, and if you want to be able to go on looking for her, you may prefer to leave her and her unpleasant friends out of your statement to him."

"Anyway, it's what *you'd* prefer, isn't it?" I said.

"I'd very much prefer it."

"All right," I said after a moment. "It's quite true; I'd prefer it, too. But may I ask you some things about Teresa?"

"You want to trade?"

"Certainly not," I said. "I just thought— well, as a matter of fact, I was going to ask you the questions anyway."

"Go ahead," he said. "Only perhaps you'd tell me first why you think I'm worth questioning on the subject of her present where-abouts. I can tell you a certain amount about her actions at the time of David's murder, but I haven't heard anything of her since, and I'm curious why you should think I might have."

So there we were again at the question that I could not answer without making a serious accusation against Nicholas Hill.

I decided that the only thing to do was to ignore it.

"You said murder," I said. "But Teresa was acquitted.

"Because she was in England," he said. "In this country it would have been a verdict of not proven."

"Which was the verdict she found had really been passed on her anyway," I said, "except by Mrs. Hill. But I don't really understand why. What is there about her that made that happen?"

"About Sheila, do you mean, or about Teresa?"

I thought for a moment. "About both of them."

Mrs. Fenwick, who had been muttering to herself in a shocked sort of way ever since I had agreed to mislead the police, said, "It's no use asking him about Sheila. He's been besotted with her for the last twenty years. She was a little girl at school when he first met her, and he made up his mind there and then that he was going to marry her when she was old enough. But Sheila herself never saw it in that way, and when her schooldays were over she went out to join her family in the Sudan and there she married Reggie Hill. And it's taken her all these years since his death to recognise that she might just as well marry Alec as have him around all the time, scaring other men off."

He sighed resignedly. "That's my mother's version of it and I suppose it always will be. However, it's not a complete picture."

"Apparently not," she said. "There's this business of buying Footfield House, for instance, of which I've heard nothing till this moment."

"Mother, I had to do it," he said. "I had to make Sheila cut loose from the past. The wretched place has hung over us all these years. Sheila wouldn't go near it, yet she wouldn't make up her mind to sell it. So I arranged for her to be offered the sort of price she really couldn't refuse—far more than it's worth. But I'd be glad for the moment if she didn't have to know that. When I gave the keys back to Mrs. Bullock, I asked her not to talk about it to anyone, and I don't think she will. She's pretty close mouthed."

"And what are you going to do with it, now that you've bought it?" Mrs. Fenwick asked.

"Pull it down!" he said with a violence that made me start.

"Good," she said. "Sometimes you have sense, Alec."

"I thought it was going to be turned into a country club," I said.

"I did consider that," he said. "But then I decided to go down and take a look at the place again. And as soon as I stepped inside, I knew the only thing was to pull it down. Flatten it to the ground. Blot out it and its memories for ever!"

His voice rasped on the last words, and suddenly I wondered if it was only the memory of David's death that was to be blotted out, or also the memory of Reggie Hill, Sheila's first husband.

"And no doubt you decided, too, that it wouldn't pay," Mrs. Fenwick said.

They exchanged a glance as a maid appeared who said that Sergeant Stuart had arrived and was asking for me.

The statement with which the sergeant presently went away was untrue in almost every particular. I had told him that I had wanted to come to Hunter Law to interview Mrs. Fenwick for an article in a series that I was writing on old houses in Scotland; that I had mentioned this to Mr. Hill, but that he had apparently forgotten the fact; that I had happened to see in a car in Edinburgh a woman whom I had met on the train the night before and with whom I had talked about the articles that I was writing; and that she and her companion had offered me a lift part of the way to Hunter Law, telling me that I should easily be able to thumb another lift for the rest of the way. And after we had parted, I had said, I had been so enchanted with the view from the top of the Lammermuir hills that I had decided to go for a short walk before trying to stop another car, had caught my foot in the heather and fallen, then had been caught in the rain. I must have been a very dreadful sight, I had agreed, when kind Mr. Grant had picked me up, but kind Mrs. Fenwick had looked after me. All was well now, and I was very sorry for the trouble that had been caused by the unnecessary anxiety of Mr. Hill.

I did not think that the sergeant really believed me, but with the calm gaze of Alexander Fenwick upon him, he did not seem inclined to say so.

When the sergeant had gone, Alec gave an abrupt laugh.

"Congratulations, Miss Purvis," he said. "That was a far better story than I was expecting. I suppose you really are a journalist, by the way?"

"No," I said, "I'm a teacher. That's to say, I'm going to start being one in a few weeks' time."

"Don't you think perhaps you've missed your vocation?"

"I used to think so," I said, "but the queer thing is, I'm beginning to feel how nice it would be to know exactly where I'm going to be for the next twenty-four hours and that all that time I could just stick to some plain facts out of a text book. I don't think I'm really a natural liar. Yet it's so easy, once one starts, that I'm rather frightened."

"In any case, I must thank you," Alec said. "As you've realised, mentioning your quest for Teresa Swale and your treatment at the hands of her friends would have mean a lot of questioning for us all, and that wouldn't have been just the pleasantest celebration of our engagement for Sheila and me."

His mother made a growling sound in her throat.

"Selfishness, that's what's the matter with you, Alec," she said. "And that's why Sheila wouldn't marry you before. She knows you're used to having your way about everything."

"Have I ever had it with Sheila?" he asked in a voice that was suddenly less assured, less equable. "But I do thank you, Miss Purvis, and to show that I do, I'll try to tell you as much as I know about Teresa Swale, and without pressing you to answer that question you don't want to answer—I mean, why you think I'm worth questioning about her."

"But I only thought . . ." I began. He held up a hand.

"If I pressed the question, I'd get an answer something like the one you've just given Stuart, shouldn't I? You've got something on your mind that you're peculiarly anxious to keep to yourself. Well, who hasn't? So go ahead now and ask me what questions you like and I promise I'll try to answer."

I felt scared of him. He was too shrewd and too forceful. Besides,

I was all of a sudden certain that he knew what I was trying to keep to myself. He knew of Nicholas's marriage to Teresa.

Staring into the log fire, I wished that we could go back to talking about peacocks being chased by foxes and other interesting things like that. But there was a job to finish.

"You were going to tell me about why you think Teresa murdered David," I said, "and why Mrs. Hill doesn't think so."

"Sheila doesn't think so because she's never really accepted the fact of murder," he said. "It was less unbearable for her to believe that David's death was an accident—cruel and avoidable, if proper care had been taken, but still without any deliberate evil behind it. That's the kind of person she is. She finds it almost impossibly difficult to believe in the worst in other people. She'd evidence before the murder that Teresa wasn't honest, and she'd talked it over with me, yet she wouldn't take any decisive action about it. She kept saying she just possibly could be wrong and that the accusation, if it was wrong, would be far worse than the dishonesty."

"You're talking about the theft of some jewellery, aren't you?" I said.

"Yes, Sheila had been missing some odds and ends of not very valuable stuff. But apart from that, and perhaps really more serious, Teresa had faked a reference to get the job. Mrs. Bullock found that out somehow and told Sheila. The reference was given by a friend of Teresa's in London, who said in a letter and confirmed it on the telephone that Teresa had worked for her for three years. But, in fact, Teresa had been working for some people in Cornwall, and she'd disappeared from their house quite suddenly without explanations just about the time that she applied for the job with Sheila. To be fair, however, they'd nothing against her honesty, and it was only after the murder, when they were questioned by the police, that they admitted they'd really been quite glad to see her go, as they'd been growing a bit disturbed about her morals and doubted if she was quite the person they wanted in charge of their child. And that was confirmed later by the police—Teresa had had affairs with several men in the neighbourhood. But there was no sign of trouble of that kind while she was at Footfield, and Sheila said there was no real proof that it was Teresa who had taken her things. There were other people who could have got at them quite easily, since Sheila never troubled to lock anything up—for instance, a new housemaid, about whom nothing much was known, and a window cleaner and some decorators. And ever since, Sheila's stuck to it that there's a big difference between stealing a few pretty things and doing a murder."

"Which is quite true, isn't it?" I said.

"Of course it is."

"So the question is, why do *you* think Teresa did the murder?"

"To begin with," Alec said, "let's clear up the fact of why I'm sure it *was* a murder."

"It was because of the chair, wasn't it?" I said.

"Yes, because of the chair from Sheila's bedroom. David's sticky finger marks were on the chair, and there was mud from his shoes on the seat of it, and there's no doubt that David had pulled it out of her room and climbed up on it himself to try to reach the pink flowers he could see at the window. But at the time when his body was found on the path below, the chair was back in Sheila's bedroom. And that confirmed part of Teresa's story. She said she'd found David climbing on the chair and had picked him up and held him out of the window to show him how far he'd fall if he tried that sort of thing, and that then she'd put the chair back in the bedroom. Suppose then that David pulled that chair out again after that and climbed up to the window and fell out: somebody must again have returned the chair to the bedroom—and why should anyone, guilty or innocent, have done that? For a guilty person, the chair under the window was the best possible defence. And an innocent person, seeing it there, would certainly have looked out of the window and given the alarm. So that means, in my opinion, that it's quite certain the chair stayed in the bedroom and that David didn't climb up to the window by himself, but was picked up and thrown out."

I did not want to dwell on the image that that conjured up

"What does Mrs. Hill say to that argument?" I asked.

"She says that perhaps Teresa found the chair under the window, looked out and saw David and panicked, and put the chair back in the bedroom, without realising what a blunder that was, and then denied everything out of terror."

"Couldn't that be true?" I asked.

"Just conceivably. But I don't believe it."

"Why not?"

I wanted to see if he would say anything at all about Teresa's motive and so possibly find out if I had been right, a few minutes before, in thinking that he knew of Teresa's marriage.

His answer cast no light on this at all.

"As much as anything, it was the woman herself," he said. "There was a soft, insinuating gentleness about her, yet at the same time a vein of violence. I don't think Sheila ever encountered it, but I'd overhead her once storming at Mrs. Bullock, because Mrs. Bullock had criticised something she'd done, and it was like a safety valve blowing on a boiler. Foul language and threats poured out of her. But the next moment she realised I was there and she was all sweetness again. I thought the whole scene horrible and I implored Sheila to get rid of her. I said that with a temper like that, anything could happen."

"And isn't that more or less what Nicholas wrote from Rome?" Mrs. Fenwick exclaimed. "He'd never met the women, yet he wrote and implored Sheila to get rid of her. Now you can't say that wasn't a remarkable case of—well, of something, can you?"

There was a slight pause before Alec answered, "No—it was remarkable."

He and I exchanged a swift look. Immediately afterwards he went on quickly, "I believe, as a matter of fact, Nick's reasons were economic. He didn't think Sheila could afford a nurse for David, if she was going to go on living in that big house with a housekeeper and two other servants. And he was perfectly right—she couldn't. But she'd next to no sense of money in those days. She was eating into capital all the time she was living at Footfield."

Mrs. Fenwick gave a snort. "Economic! Miss Purvis and I know better than that. Nicholas has a gift."

"Did he come immediately after the murder?" I asked.

"Yes," Alec answered. "Sheila telephoned and he started back the same night. He'd have been returning in a month or two anyway. He was out there on a scholarship, you know. It was for a year, but he stayed and got a job in an architect's office in London."

"And Roy Carney—did he come back then, too?" I asked.

"Roy——? Oh, you mean Bill Bullock. I'd forgotten about his being in Rome with Nick, but he was, of course. He'd gone out there to write a novel, I believe. He'd already written one, and he went out to Italy on the proceeds to write the next. And so on. He's always done a lot of travelling. For backgrounds and so on, I suppose. I can't say I read his books myself. No, I don't think he came home with Nick."

From the careful lack of expression in his tone, I guessed that he did not like Roy Carney. I realised that I should have been surprised if he had. They were two successful men, but in ways so different that Alec was bound, I thought, to regard the other with suspicion, as if he were getting away with something to which he had no right.

"Did the police ever hear about that letter from Rome?" I asked.

Alec hesitated and, for the first time, seemed unwilling to answer. Then he said abruptly, "We accepted Nick's statement that he'd never met Teresa, and we knew for certain that he was in Rome at the time of David's death, and in any case Sheila hadn't kept the letter. So we agreed between us to forget it, as it could only have made serious trouble for Nick. Now is there anything else you want to know?"

Something that he had said had started my mind racing, but it was on the subject of Nicholas and his marriage to Teresa, and although I felt certain by now that Alec knew of this marriage, I felt as strongly as ever that I did not want to discuss it with him.

"If you haven't heard anything of Teresa recently," I said, "there's really nothing else to ask, unless you've any idea where she might have gone to."

"I've no idea at all," he said. "And now I'd like to ask you something. Why have you been asking me all these questions about what happened five years ago? Have you got some idea into your head that you're going to solve the problem of poor little David's death?"

His eyes mocked me for my youth, my ignorance, and presumption.

I met them as confidently as I was able. But before I had to try to answer his question, we heard voices outside the door. It opened, and Sheila Hill came in, followed by Nicholas and Roy Carney.

CHAPTER THIRTEEN

I wished it had not happened at just that moment. I was not ready to meet either Nicholas or Roy. But here they all were, looking at me as if I were as strange a creature to find eating boiled eggs in that drawing room, in my velvet dressing gown and striped pyjamas, as if it were the peacock that had come into tea.

Roy hung back behind the other two, with a diffidence I had never seen in him before, as if he were unsure of his welcome. There was something else about him I had not seen before, a tension, an air of only half-hidden hostility to somebody, or perhaps to everybody there.

I could not think what he was doing here. He must have flown from London to Edinburgh. But why?

His eyes met mine across the room, but only for a moment, before he turned them with peculiar intensity on Alexander Fenwick.

But Alec had eyes only for Sheila. She had come into the room with the same buoyancy and the radiance in her face that I had seen in the morning. Alexander Fenwick was far from my own idea of the

132

perfect sort of man to marry, because he would always be inclined to run the life of everyone around him with a strong-minded competence, which on my sort of character would have a perfectly paralyzing effect. But to Sheila it seemed to promise sunny peace.

Though it was to me that she spoke as she came in, she went straight to Alec's side and slipped a hand through his arm.

"I brought them both as quickly as I could," she said to me, gesturing at Roy and Nicholas, "and we've brought your suitcase and your handbag. And I'm so glad you got here safely, though none of us understand exactly how it happened. Nicholas said you've been kidnapped, but of course that wasn't true, was it?" She looked at Alec. "Did you see any kidnappers, darling?"

There was light mockery in her tone, at which, I was interested to see, Nicholas flushed and hard lines tightened about his mouth.

"Miss Purvis parted company with them somewhere up on the Lammermuirs," Alec answered. "She was brought the rest of the way by Archie Grant. And we've agreed now, for the benefit of the police, that there weren't any kidnappers and that the matter's closed." He turned to the other two men. "Hullo, Nick. And you're Bullock, aren't you? It's a long time since we met." His tone to both of them was casual, neither warm nor cold.

"I'd sooner hear what happened from Elspeth herself," Nicholas said. He came towards me. "I saw your face in that car and I found your handbag left behind in the flat. You didn't go willingly, did you?"

"Running out on you again?" I said. "No, Nick, I wasn't doing that."

"Then why does Alec say the matter's closed?" he asked.

"Well, that's what we agreed," I said. "It's quite all right. And if you've brought my clothes, I think I'd like to get dressed properly; then I could go back to Edinburgh and catch a train home."

"I want to know what happened first," he said.

Alec had put his arm round Sheila's shoulders. "I think Nick believes I somehow intimidated you into silence, Miss Purvis," he said. "But if anything, Nick, it was the other way round. Miss

Purvis made me tell her all sorts of things I'd no intention of talking about at all."

"And I've got in everyone's way quite enough," I said. "You've all been very kind, but if there's a bus back to Edinburgh . . ."

From behind Nicholas, Roy Carney said, "If you want to leave, Elspeth, I'll go back to Edinburgh with you. I don't think my presence here is particularly useful to anybody."

I turned to Mrs. Fenwick and was going to ask her where I could dress, but she had just turned to Sheila, holding both her hands out to her, and I remembered that this was the first time that the two of them had met since Sheila had become engaged to marry Alec. Deciding to leave them to one another, I muttered that I would get dressed, and went out into the hall, where I saw my suitcase and handbag.

I did not know what room had been prepared for me, but I thought that I could dress in the bathroom. I was stooping to pick up my suitcase when I found Roy standing beside me.

His manner was still tense and strange and his face rather white, as if he were either scared or exceedingly angry.

"Are we going or staying?" he asked.

"I think I'm going, but that doesn't mean you've got to," I said. "Why did you come here?"

"Because I told him to." It was Nicholas's voice. He had come out just after Roy and now stepped forward between us. "I'd just finished telephoning him when I saw you go by in that car. I didn't want him to leave the country without the two of you meeting once more."

His tone, harsh with anger, was as strange as Roy's.

"Leave the country?" I said uncertainly. "When?"

"I'm leaving from Prestwick tonight," Roy answered, "so I haven't got a great deal of time to spare. If you're coming back to Edinburgh with me, you'd better hurry."

"She's not going back to Edinburgh with you," Nicholas said. "If she goes at all, it'll be with me. But before that, you're going to tell her the truth."

"What do you want me to tell her the truth about, Nick?" With

a swift look over his shoulder at the drawing-room door, Roy
dropped his voice. "You? Teresa? I understood she knew that already."

"About you, damn you—if you remember what the truth is!"
Nick said, also barely above a whisper.

Roy gave a small, tight-lipped smile. "Perhaps I don't, Nick."

"Then you'd better start trying to."

They exchanged one of those intimate, understanding glances
which I had first seen in Roy's hotel in London. Now I wondered
how I could ever have mistaken it for a glance of friendship. For
the truth was that these two hated each other. That was clear now.

Roy, who was far the quicker of the two, saw this dawn upon me.
He put a hand on my shoulder.

"She isn't as innocent as she looks, is she, Nick? You may find
she's got it all thought out already. Then I needn't say anything,
need I? I can just go and catch my plane."

"You're going to tell the truth," Nicholas said. "Here and now."

"Are you sure that's really what you want? Mightn't it be better to
leave it as it is? If she likes you as much as you obviously like her,
she's probably got it all worked out that Teresa got you into her
clutches. So why trouble to correct that impression?"

Fury blazed in Nicholas's dark eyes, and at the sight of it Roy
smiled again. With every moment his self-possession was growing,
just as Nicholas was losing his.

"You see, Elspeth," Roy went on, "Nicholas wants me to tell
you that he isn't really married to Teresa at all. I'm not sure why he
wants me to tell you this, because you went to Somerset House
yourself, didn't you? You saw the marriage certificate. So if he
really isn't married to Teresa at all, there could only be one reason,
couldn't there? Which is that he was already married to somebody
else. . . . Oh no, there could be one other reason!" He went a step
closer to Nicholas. There was a sparkle of excitement in the grey
eyes under the sun-bleached eyebrows. "And that reason, Nick, is
that you happen to know Teresa's dead. Perhaps what you see before you, Elspeth, is a sorrowing widower."

There was bewilderment now, as well as rage, on Nicholas's face.

I felt sick and frightened, because I felt in my bones, without experience, that this was a combination that could only explode into violence. And Roy was ready for it, for some reason wanting it, trying to provoke it.

As I saw Nicholas's hands come up, I heard my own voice say shrilly, "No, there's another reason! The one Nick wants you to tell me—but you needn't—because I *have* got it all thought out already. Nick never married Teresa at all. It was you who married her!"

As they both turned to look at me, for an instant forgetting each other, I grasped my suitcase, clutched the purple dressing gown around me, shot up the stairs to the bathroom, closed the door behind me, and locked it.

I dressed as fast as I could. But my hands were shaking, and the more I tried to hurry, the more perversely my clothes twisted themselves up about me. I laddered a pair of stockings. The zip on my skirt stuck and I caught myself putting my jumper on back to front.

All the time, I knew that there was no good reason for the hurry. I still meant to go back to Edinburgh and catch a train home to London, but first I wanted to say good-bye to Mrs. Fenwick, and to thank her for her kindness, and to rescue the clothes that she had taken away to dry. And perhaps I wanted to talk to Nicholas, though whether or not I did rather depended on him.

In any case, I knew that it would have been a good idea to take my time and calm down, only the violence that there had been for those few minutes between the two men had somehow upset me almost as much as if it had all been directed against me, and my fumbling haste was a senseless way of trying to escape from it.

In the end I managed to get myself tidily dressed. Then I opened the door quietly and went out. The hall below was empty. But as I went down the stairs, I saw Nicholas outside in the garden, walking up and down.

He had been waiting for me and, as soon as he saw me, he came to the door.

"He's gone," he said. "Elspeth——" There was anxiety on his face and the same bewilderment that had been there before, but the rage had died. "You *can't* have guessed what really happened."

"Wasn't I right?" I said.

He lifted his hands and dropped them. "Yes, but I thought you only said it to calm us down. In another moment . . . Roy's always known how to tie me up in knots; then I lose my temper. It's a rotten habit."

"I know. You thought you'd got him on the defensive and instead he attacked you and you couldn't think fast enough to keep up." I stepped out into the portico beside him. The sunshine lay clear and golden on the grass slopes outside. "Let's go for a walk," I said.

In surprise he looked down at my feet. "In those?"

I was wearing my bedroom slippers, because, when I had packed in London, it had not occurred to me to pack a spare pair of shoes.

"A short walk," I said, "just to be somewhere quiet. I seem to have been asking or answering questions all day."

He turned and we started down the drive together.

We walked slowly, because my foot still hurt. Besides, we were not going anywhere in particular. The afternoon sky was a deep blue, the hills that met it were an even deeper blue, and there was a sweet resiny scent in the air, which came from a grove of fir trees opposite the gate at the end of the drive. We wandered a little way in among these trees, then sat down side by side on a fallen log. Between the thick, copper-coloured trunks of the firs, we could see the sparkle of water rippling between mossy stones.

Nicholas sat and gazed at me with a dreamy, bemused concentration while I told him of my experience with Callie and Lance. He muttered at the stupidity of my having lied to the police about it, then said that perhaps it had been the best thing to do; then he said abruptly, "I suppose it was Alec who told you the truth about that marriage?"

"Not a word," I said. "But I guessed he knew. How did he find out?"

"I consulted him. But the question is, how did you find out?"

"I think I've been getting there little by little," I said, "ever since I went to Footfield. I saw the clematis there at the window and that reminded me that David died in May. And the date of Teresa's marriage was in January. At the time that didn't mean anything to me. But then you told me about going to Rome for a year, and a little while ago Mr. Fenwick corroborated that and said that the year was nearly over when you came back. So I began to wonder how you could have been in Cornwall in January to marry Teresa without anyone knowing, because the police would have examined your passport when they were checking your alibi; and somehow I think that if you'd spent a few unexplained days in England, your movements then would have been rather carefully investigated. And if they'd taken you to Cornwall—well, someone surely would have remembered seeing you with Teresa."

I looked at him questioningly and he gave a slight nod, but did not say anything.

I went on, "But it was really just as if there hadn't been any contact between you—except for the letter you wrote Sheila, telling her to get rid of Teresa, which Mrs. Fenwick thought was precognition and Alec tried to explain away as economic advice to Sheila. But he happened to remind me of something you'd said—that Roy was with you about the time that letter was written. And also he told me that Roy didn't come back with you when you came home. The awfully good, loyal friend, who was almost a brother and who was staying with you when this frightful thing happened, didn't stand by you then. He faded out, and so far as I've been able to make out, didn't come back to England until a few days ago. And his mother hadn't any of his books in her sitting room, and the people in the village didn't seem to know he was a successful writer —so it looked as if she'd reasons for keeping very quiet about him. And that reason was that it was really Roy who married Teresa, wasn't it? Roy pretending to be Nicholas Hill, then hiding from the wife he'd abandoned."

Nicholas nodded again, then started to speak quickly. "You know Roy a little, so you ought to be able to understand how it happened. He'd rather a way, you see, of pretending to be me when he was among strangers. It sounds funny enough now, but he grew up with the feeling that it was a terrific thing to be a Hill of Footfield House. And, of course, Footfield House, when he talked about it, became several times the size it really was, and the number of servants was trebled, and our one old Austin Twelve became two Rolls Bentleys. I've always thought it was mainly his mother's fault. Instead of letting us just be friends in our own way, which would have meant his pushing me around quite happily, because he always had twice the brains I had, she was always telling him what a privilege it was for him to know me at all, and that he must always remember that when he grew up I'd be rich and could do what I liked, but he'd have to work hard for his living. And so on. All of which, as I said, has its own grim humour now, apart from the facts that it sickened me, even when I was twelve years old, and damaged Roy for life. From that day to this, I don't believe he's ever learnt the difference between what's true and what he'd like to be true. So when he decided to go away to Cornwall to try to write a novel, and when he got picked up by a nice-looking girl there, it was quite normal for him to say he was Nicholas Hill and to spin his yarn about Footfield House and the two Rolls Bentleys."

"Which I suppose made Teresa concentrate on marriage," I said.

"Yes. But, of course, as soon as she began to wonder why the marriage had to be kept secret and why the rich heir of Footfield expected her to stay in her job and didn't give her any money, Roy thought it was time to leave. He never liked to have a fantasy blow up in his face. So as soon as he finished the book, he told Teresa he was going to London to see a literary agent, and thereupon faded out of her life. And it was quite typical of him that he never dreamt she might throw up her job and go to Footfield herself. Roy's dreamworld hasn't any past or any future."

"But why didn't Teresa find out the truth straight away in Footfield?"

"Because naturally she inquired for me and was told I'd been away in Rome for months. So then she realised she'd been told a good many lies and she worked out her own version of the truth, which unfortunately happened to be quite wrong. I got this out of her in the only conversation I ever had with her. She decided that her husband had been sent out to Rome by his family, for reasons connected with swindling him out of his rights, but that he'd returned secretly and had been hiding in Cornwall until a propitious moment for taking action of some sort. She was an awfully ignorant girl and her view of life was almost as melodramatic as Roy's—and, anyway, she thought that if she applied for the job of nurse to David, which Sheila was advertising at the time, she'd have as good a chance as any of tracking her husband down again without having to spend money or get the police in on the job. And as soon as she got there, she realised from photographs about the place that the man she'd married was Bill Bullock, the son of the housekeeper. But no one could tell her where he was or when he was likely to be back again."

"And Roy had gone out to Rome to tell you about it?"

"To tell me about it and see if I could get him out of the mess, which was what he generally counted on when things got too difficult."

"Didn't he care for Teresa at all? Didn't he even think of telling her the truth and sticking to her?"

"When he'd just got his first book accepted, and got a contract which seemed to him to promise riches—if he hadn't got a wife to support? On one subject, and that's the making and spending of money, Roy's always been astonishingly realistic."

"So you wrote that letter for him, urging Sheila to get rid of Teresa."

"Oh no, I didn't," Nicholas said.

"But Mrs. Fenwick said . . . And Alec . . ."

He shook his head. "What I told Roy was that he'd taken something on and he'd better see it through for once. I knew nothing about the letter till I got Sheila's answer to it, which said curtly that Teresa was perfectly satisfactory and she couldn't see what I was so steamed up about."

"So forgery's among Roy's talents, too."

"Well, he typed the letter and dashed off something like my signature at the end of it, but I don't suppose it would ever have stood up to examination. But Sheila just threw the letter away. I gave Roy hell about the whole thing, and he turned on me, just as he did today, and told me it was really all my fault, because it had been my idea that he might use his imagination to some purpose by writing a book, and he'd never have met Teresa at all if I hadn't lent him some money and sent him off by himself to do it. And while I was trying to think that one out—because somehow I never could get rid of a feeling of responsibility for him, even when I knew it was damned nonsense—we got Sheila's telephone call about David. She told me that Teresa was suspected and asked me what I'd really meant in my letter. And I swore to her solemnly that I'd never met Teresa in my life and implored her to say nothing to anyone about the letter until I'd talked to her. And because I was Reggie's brother, she agreed. Then I talked to Roy, saying we'd better go straight back to England together, and he threw a kind of brainstorm, saying he'd kill himself if he was dragged into the mess. So I—I said I'd see what I could do to keep him out of it. Then he packed up and disappeared. And actually that's the last I saw of him until last Monday, though I heard from him occasionally when he started to become successful. But, you may have noticed, no photographs of him are ever published, and the little biographies of him on his paperbacks are complete fiction. So an ignorant girl like Teresa hadn't much chance of tracking him down."

"And how did you explain the letter to Sheila in the end?" I asked.

"I left it to Alec. He was staying there and I told him the truth about everything. He's a tough, clearheaded character and he thought up the economic explanation and managed to make her believe it."

"But why didn't he simply advise you to tell the truth about Roy?" I asked.

"He did—only by then I'd committed myself not to, except in the last resort."

"But why, why, why?" I cried. "Whyever did you do such a crazy thing?"

In my exasperation I pounded my knees with my fists. Nicholas suddenly reached out and took both my hands in his and drew me round to face him. He tried to say something, but the words seemed to stick. There was an anxious, helpless look on his face which all at once I couldn't bear to see there, so without quite knowing what I was going to do, I leant towards him and laid my cheek against his and said, "It's all right, it's all right, you've already told me. You thought even Roy didn't deserve Teresa."

He went very still; then his arms went round me and we held each other tightly. But it was only for a moment; then he stood up and took a couple of steps away from me. Turning, he faced me again.

"And you see, I was innocent enough to believe that threat of suicide, because it would have been the end of Roy if the whole story had come out," he said. "The woman he'd married had gone to Footfield and murdered the child. She'd gone there because of Roy's lies. And, as you said, I thought even Roy didn't deserve such a punishment. So we thought that if neither of us said anything, just possibly nothing need come out. Hill isn't an uncommon name. And we did get away with it, mainly because Teresa herself had to keep quiet about it for her own safety. The one thing we never dreamt of was that she'd be acquitted because of our silence. And now, well, I'm afraid we're going to hear more of her soon and that it may mean trouble."

I wanted to get up quickly and cross the short distance that he had put between us.

"Why?" I asked.

"Because I think Roy knows where she is and what she's been doing." Nicholas looked at me with an odd air of apology. "Her husband's family, you see, Elspeth, didn't mean Sheila. It meant Mrs. Bullock."

I felt a chill begin to creep over me. "And you knew that all along."

"Of course I did."

"Of course. And it's why you were sure we shouldn't find her in Edinburgh."

"It's also why Roy told Mrs. Bullock to tell you all you wanted to know about Sheila," Nicholas said. "They wanted to send you on a wild-goose chase to Scotland, so that Roy could meet Teresa in peace."

"Did he actually tell you that?" I asked.

"No," he said. "He never admitted knowing where she was. But I think that's what must have happened. He did tell me he'd come to England because his mother cabled that Teresa had just been to see her, saying she knew now that her husband was the successful writer, Roy Carney, and that she intended to be well paid for keeping her mouth shut. As you know, Roy went to the address she'd given Mrs. Bullock, but she wasn't there. That's more or less all he told me. But I think he must have seen Teresa last night and fixed up some agreement with her, and that's why he's able to leave the country again today."

"Then you knew he didn't mean to watch for me at London Airport," I said.

"Yes, I did."

"But suppose I'd gone by plane. It's almost looks, you know, as if he wanted you out of the way, too. I suppose it was he who suggested you should keep a watch for me at Kings Cross."

He nodded. He had propped his back against the trunk of a fir tree and put his hands in his pockets. The small distance between us seemed to be growing longer with every moment.

"How did Teresa find out that Billie Bullock was Roy Carney?" I asked.

"Your brother-in-law told her," Nicholas said. "It was on one of the tapes Roy took from the Lincolns' flat. She mentioned Bill Bullock quite casually in her story, and Lincoln asked her if she knew that he'd turned into Roy Carney."

So that was how it had all begun. Bernard was the sort of man who always knew things like that. He seemed to know a little about almost everybody in the writing and publishing world. But, of course, he had not realised what he was doing when he gave the information away to Teresa.

"Suppose Teresa hadn't been acquitted," I said, "don't you think she'd have dragged Roy into it, once she knew things were hopeless for her?"

"I suppose she might have."

"And wouldn't you have got into a lot of trouble for suppressing evidence, or something?"

Nicholas gave a wry smile. "I was five years younger than I am now. I had some odd ideas about friendship."

"And Roy could twist you round his finger." I stood up. "Well, now I'd better think of getting back to London. I seem to have wasted a lot of time here."

I said it bitterly, but that was far more because of the swiftness with which Nicholas had withdrawn from my impulsive show of sympathy, or whatever it had been, than because of my wasted time. After all, he had not advised me to go to Edinburgh and he had told me repeatedly that I should not find Teresa there. I had no reason to be bitter with him because of my own blunders. Or for the other reason either, if it came to that. Some people had no use for sympathy, particularly sympathy which they had not asked for.

I started to walk back through the trees towards the road. Nicholas waited until I was well ahead of him; then he followed me slowly, drawing level with me only as we crossed the road and walking up the drive at my side. There was an aimlessness about him now, as if, after all that talking, he had not the faintest idea what to do next.

I knew what I meant to do. I meant to get back to Edinburgh as fast as possible.

But this turned out to be more difficult than I had imagined, because, when I saw Mrs. Fenwick and told her that I really must return to London, she seemed to think that it would be a serious failure of hospitality to allow me to travel by bus, particularly in bedroom slippers. If I insisted on returning to London that night, she said, Alec would drive me to Edinburgh. So there was no reason for hurry. I could stay for a drink and a meal, and be in plenty of time for one of the late trains.

That was how I happened to be sitting in the Fenwicks' drawing room, with a glass of sherry in my hand, when the six o'clock news was switched on and I heard that the body of a woman, identified as that of Teresa Swale, who, listeners were reminded, had been acquitted five years before of the murder of David Hill, had been found in a black trunk in her own room in Bloomsbury. She had been dead for at least ten days. The police were looking for a woman called Caroline Mars and a man called Lance Martin, who, it was said, they thought might be able to help them in their inquiries.

CHAPTER FOURTEEN

I remembered the black trunk. I remembered looking at it indifferently, only wondering a little about the initials on it and taking far more interest in the drawers that the landlady had been opening and closing.

She had not suggested opening the black trunk. She had not gone near it. But if it was true now that Teresa had been dead for at least ten days, her body had been there inside the trunk while the old woman was showing me the room.

I could not stand the image that rose in my mind at that thought, and I shut my eyes tightly. But the image only became sharper, so I opened them again and saw Sheila raise her head and dab at her eyes. At the sudden sound of Teresa's name in the calm B.B.C. voice, she had given a little moan; then, when Alec went to her and put his arms round her, she had clutched him with both hands and hidden her face against him.

"I don't know why I'm crying," she said. "It isn't for her. I'm glad she's dead."

Alec's hand gently stroked her hair.

She went on shakily, "The trunk—it sounds like the one I sent her belongings on to her in, after the trial. It belonged to Reggie. There's a sort of poetic justice in that. I know I always said I didn't believe she killed David. That she was going about safely and she'd done that—I couldn't face it. Because if she had, I'd have had to kill her myself. But now she's dead. . . . And I'm so glad, so glad."

"Only her murderers happen to be loose in this neighbourhood," Mrs. Fenwick said drily—"a fact about which Alec and Miss Purvis conspired together to deceive the police. That seems rather unfortunate at the moment."

"I'm not sure," Alec said thoughtfully. "I'm not at all sure it wasn't an extraordinary stroke of luck."

"If you mean that you don't intend to tell the truth now . . ." his mother said. She turned to me. "Don't listen to him this time. Tell the truth about the whole business and stick to it."

"I though there hadn't been any persuasion," Nicholas said. "I thought the story Elspeth told the police here was her own idea."

"Wait a moment," Alec said impatiently. "Let me think. I don't believe there's any need for any of us to say anything at all."

The tweed-covered bulk of Mrs. Fenwick shot up out of her chair. She came trotting across the room to me and grasped my arm.

"I've been law-abiding all my life and I'm sure you have, too, and this is murder," she said. "If you don't tell the truth about that horrible pair, I'm going to; but I don't imagine you're even thinking of concealing it any longer, are you?"

Sheila raised her head again. "It's the murder of a murderess—and I'm grateful to the people who did it. I don't see why any of us should say anything about them, at least until we're asked."

"The only thing is, they didn't murder her," I said.

There was a stir in the room—the small sort of stir made by people catching their breaths, turning a little, then becoming still.

I did not like the stillness, or the feeling of so many eyes upon me. I went on, "They kidnapped me this morning because they thought I knew where Teresa was. They tried to make me tell them.

147

They thought they could get hold of the money they thought she was going to get from you. And when I managed to persuade them I didn't know where she was, they let me go."

"Then there's even less need to say anything about them," Alec said. "And who's to know that we listened to the news just now? You can leave for London, as you intended, and, like us, read about the murder in tomorrow's newspaper."

"I don't know what's got into you, Alec, and I won't put up with it," Mrs. Fenwick said fiercely. "I've always told the truth so far as I was able and I can't see why I should stop now, of all times."

"Because one truth leads to another," her son said.

Not understanding in the least, she gave an angry snort.

He had not meant her to understand him. It was to me that he had spoken, warning me that once I started to tell the truth about why I and Callie and Lance had come hunting for Teresa in Scotland, the truth would be out about Nicholas's supposed marriage to her.

Yes, but why should it not come out now? I turned and looked at Nicholas.

"At any rate, if she's been dead for ten days, Roy had nothing to do with it," he said. "He landed in England only three days ago, and Teresa was dead by then."

"Roy?" Sheila said in a puzzled way. "Why should he have anything to do with it?"

"I'm going to tell you," Nicholas answered. "I rather wish I'd done it long ago, instead of waiting till I'd no choice—because once the police catch up with Martin and the Mars woman, they're going to tell as much as they know. And the whole story's better than half the story. But I'd still like Roy to have a chance to get clear, which is what he seems very anxious to do. And if Elspeth does as Alec suggests and goes back to London tonight, Roy can probably get out of the country before any of us has to tell the police anything."

I was going to protest that I had no intention now of returning to London that night, when suddenly, with extraordinary clarity, I remembered that moment in the car with Callie and Lance, when telling them the truth had done nothing for me, but Leni Briefbach had saved me.

So I said nothing and, as Nicholas started to tell Sheila the story that he had told me under the fir trees, I decided that I would do as he asked. I would go back to London that night and know nothing about Teresa's murder until the morning.

I suppose I might actually have done this if, before Nicholas's story was finished, there had not been the sound of excited voices in the hall. A flustered maid opened the door and tried to speak to Mrs. Fenwick. But she was thrust out of the way by Lance Martin, who strode into the room, followed by Callie.

They ignored everyone in the room but me.

"You!" Lance said in a voice that rasped with rage and fear. "You're the one who started all this. You came to Callie and pulled her in on this. You're the one who knows we'd nothing to do with any of it."

That was as far as he got before Alec and Nicholas moved up on either side of him.

Lance made no attempt at resistance as each of them grasped one of his arms. But Callie thrust swiftly past them into the room and strode up to me.

"Yes, it was you who came to us with the story of the money that was coming to Teresa," she said in her preposterously lady-like tones. "You got us trying to find out what really happened to Teresa. You got us driving about the country as if we were running away from something. You knew how that would look when they found Teresa. And your friends here—the ones who were frightened of Teresa—they knew that, too, when they sent you. And Lance and I, living so quietly and happily—after all the troubles I've had in my life—Lance and I, sticking together and doing nobody any harm—keeping a home going, looking after my plants—a nice, quiet couple like us!" She gave a choking wail and burst into tears, then suddenly flung her arms round my neck and clung to me. "You'll tell them it isn't true," she sobbed. "You'll tell them, won't you?"

With ferocious dignity, Mrs. Fenwick said, "Miss Mars, if that's who you are, it may interest you and your friend to learn that that's what Miss Purvis has already done. In spite of your atrocious treatment of her this morning, she gave it as her opinion, only a few minutes ago, that you and your friend had had nothing to do with the murder of Teresa Swale. Meeting the two of you face to face, however, I find it difficult to believe her. May I ask how you knew she was here?"

Callie let go of me. "We've been watching this place most of the day and we saw her driven up," she said. "We told her we were going back to Edinburgh, but when we left her up there on the moors, we came here. That's why Lance knocked her out—so that she wouldn't see which way we went. And we've been watching and searching and asking questions about Teresa, because we were sure you'd got her here, alive or dead. And all the time, it was just a trap—that's what it was, a trap!"

"Shut up, Callie!" Lance said. He turned his head towards Sheila. "You're the one who lost the kid, aren't you? D'you want to know who killed him? Because that's the one Teresa went to see. That's the one who killed her, not Callie or me." He jerked his head towards Nicholas. "Ask him what he knows."

Sheila might not have heard him, and her quiet walking to the door might have had nothing to do with what he said. There was a frozen look of shock on her face. It had first appeared while she was listening to Nicholas. She looked neither at Lance nor at anyone else as she went out. A moment later we all heard the tinkle of the telephone bell as the receiver was lifted.

Alec let go of Lance's arm.

"Mrs. Hill now knows what, as it happens, I've known all this time," he said.

I do not know why it had taken me until then to realise that Alec, knowing for all these years of Teresa's marriage, had never believed Nicholas's story that it had been Roy who had married her, any more than Sheila believed it now. All along it was Nicholas whom Alec had been shielding. Believing that it was Nicholas who had married Teresa, but that he had been ignorant of Teresa's plan to murder David, Alec had done what he could to save for Sheila some remnant of faith in the human race.

Or had there been some other reason for his silence? Had nobody yet thought of the real motive for that murder? Had nobody even begun yet to understand what had really happened?

"I've telephoned the police," Sheila said, reappearing in the doorway. "They're on their way here. They'd better be told everything."

She went out again, and I heard her start to mount the stairs.

Alec took a couple of swift steps after her, but his mother said sharply, "No, Alec! Leave her to herself now."

He stood there a moment uncertainly, then came back into the room and closed the door. As he did so, Lance jerked round. His hand went to his pocket and the knife that I had always known he had there came out, glittering.

"Get out of the way—we aren't waiting here for the police," he said.

Nicholas and Alec acted together. Callie screamed. The knife flew up to the ceiling, then fell with a thud on the carpet. Lance nursed his wrist and started to curse in a soft, spiteful monotone. Mrs. Fenwick pounced on the knife and looked at it with interest.

"I wonder how Teresa was killed," she said. "Was she stabbed? Did she have her throat cut?"

With a certain air of respect, she put the knife on the mantelpiece, in front of a clock with a pretty enamel face, supported by gilt cupids.

But Teresa had not been killed by that knife. She had been killed by a heavy blow on the head with a blunt instrument. We learnt that from Sergeant Stuart when, a few minutes later, he reappeared in the Fenwicks' house. This time he did not come alone and he did not go away again after only a short chat. He stayed for several hours, and so did the detectives who arrived after him and who questioned us all one by one and over and over again, then at last took Callie and Lance away with them, saying that they would probably be back in the morning.

It was almost midnight by then, a northern midnight, eerie to me because it was not quite dark. As I walked out of the house onto the terrace, to get away from the voices and the tired faces, which all seemed to have set into masks of hostility to one another and particularly to me, I saw that there was still a band of dusky copper along the horizon and that the sky above it had the greenish tinge of twilight.

Walking along the terrace, I found that there was a scent of roses in the cool air and that some bird was singing in the shadows. It had a sweet bubbling song. Knowing that it wasn't a nightingale, I wondered what it was, and I was standing still, listening, when Nicholas joined me. Until the singing stopped, neither of us spoke.

Then he said, "I don't think any of them believe me, Elspeth. They think I've arranged with Roy to put the blame on him, while he clears out."

"D'you think he'll get away now?" I asked. "They'll stop him at Prestwick, won't they?"

"I'm afraid so. Elspeth—what do you believe about me?"

"Perhaps it isn't very important," I said.

As he had done when we were sitting on the fallen log among the fir trees, he caught my hands and pulled me round to face him.

"It's important," he said. "You believed me before. Why don't you now?"

His face was close to mine and I could see it clearly in that curious green dusk. I saw the anxious lines and the bewilderment and, just as had happened before, I was suddenly moved by something very strong that I did not understand and I leant towards him, only this time our lips met and, when we clung together, he did not thrust me away. In the end I did not say anything at all about believing or not believing him, and presently we went back to the house in silence.

As I went up to the room that had been made ready for me in the afternoon, I felt as if I were too tired for sleep and as if everything that had happened that day would go on churning round and round in my mind all night and perhaps for ever after. Yet I think I fell asleep as soon as I lay down in the bed. Exhaustion came over me in a black tide, like an anaesthetic, and down I went into unconciousness, dreamless and complete, until a maid woke me in the morning, pulling back curtains to let in bright sunshine and putting a tea tray down on the table beside my bed. The gentleman from London, she said as she went out, would be here in half an hour.

I guessed that the gentleman was more police. Scotland Yard, perhaps. At the same time, I realised that I was incredibly hungry. During the questioning of the evening before, a cold supper of sorts had appeared, but I had not wanted to eat. But now the idea that I might have to endure more questioning before I had had breakfast seemed outrageous, and I drank my tea quickly, jumped out of bed, got dressed and went downstairs in search of food.

There was no cause for anxiety. Breakfast was laid in the dining room, and Mrs. Fenwick was there before me, ready to heap my plate with bacon and eggs. But she was grim and silent, except that now and then she muttered explosively to herself, seeming to be accusing herself of every sort of shortsightedness and stupidity. But it was not until she had finished her breakfast and lit a cigarette, over which she coughed and choked, as if smoking were something to which she was not really accustomed, but turned to only in desperation, that I found out the cause of her self-disgust.

"To have known my son all this time and not known that he was capable of such lightheadedness!" she exclaimed all of a sudden. "Concealing that woman's marriage, not only from the police, but from Sheila! Inducing you to lie to the police! Thinking that we needn't inform the police that we knew that gangster and his woman were loose in Scotland, until Sheila went and telephoned the police herself! What sort of man is it that does things like that? What's going in in his head?"

She went on, "Of course he's a Borderer, and they've always been a law unto themselves. And he's a businessman and inclined to think there are always strings that can be pulled. And he's my son, which I have to admit has probably made him a romantic. And he'd do anything in the world to protect Sheila, and he's never realised that there's a toughness in that girl which doesn't want to be protected. And that, I believe, is the real reason, whatever else she may have said, why she wouldn't marry him before. After all, most people agree that it's better for a child to have a stepfather than no father at all, and she could have kept Footfield for the boy, if she thought that was so important. But what she couldn't face was Alec's certainty that he always knows better than anyone else what ought to be done. Well, if she marries him now, he'll be lucky. It's very difficult to forgive people who've taken it on themselves to keep from you things you'd far sooner have known. Or that you *think* you'd far sooner have known. Sheila may have forgotten by now how very little more she could have borne, five years ago, than she had to bear."

She talked on, between sharp puffs at her cigarette, obviously not wanting any answer from me, until a car drove up to the house and she got up and went off at her steady trot to meet the gentleman from London.

He was a fresh-faced, heavily built man of about thirty-five, and he was from Scotland Yard, but was not, as it turned out, anyone very exalted. I think he was a sergeant. And he had not come to put the whole household through the questioning that we had endured the evening before, but for a far simpler purpose.

It was Sheila whom he wanted to see. While he waited for her, he drank coffee and talked about the weather and his garden in Finchley in a voice with a touch of the West Country in it. He was not to be drawn on the murder. His sweet peas were doing nicely, but he was afraid there was black spot on his Frenshams. When Sheila came in, followed by Alec and, a moment afterwards, by Nicholas, they all talked gardening for a minute or two, as if this were a social occasion and none of them quite knew yet who the others were.

Then at last the sergeant put a hand in his pocket, brought out a small cardboard box, opened it, and emptied its contents onto the table. They glittered there, a little heap of jewellery.

"Would you mind looking at these, Mrs. Hill," he said, "and telling me if you've ever seen them before?"

Sheila moved forward and bent over the table. Her face was grey and tired and her eyes were dull. She looked as if she had not slept at all.

"Yes," she said after a moment, "they're mine. But I lost them a long time ago. I reported that to the police at the—the time of my son's death. But they never found any trace of them."

From where I stood, at some distance from the table, I could see that there was a topaz pendant on a thin gold chain, a garnet brooch, and an opal ring, all old-fashioned and not very valuable, but charming. If they had belonged to me and I had lost them, I should have been very angry. But their loss had been such a small part of Sheila's disaster that even now she seemed to feel no interest in their recovery.

It was Alec, assuming that air of taking charge, which he seemed unable to control, who said, "Where were they found?"

"Teresa Swale had them," the man from Scotland Yard answered. "They were found yesterday, when her room was searched, after the discovery of her body."

"So she did take them," Alec said. "We always thought so, though we never knew for sure. She must have hidden them very carefully."

"Possibly someone kept them for her until after the trial," the sergeant said. "Lately, I suppose, she thought they'd been forgotten. They weren't hidden. They were in a box in her chest of drawers, with a few odd bits of Woolworth jewellery." He began to replace the pieces in the box in which he had brought them. "You'll get these back eventually, Mrs. Hill, but for the moment we'll have to hold them."

"I don't want them," Sheila said tonelessly, and turned away.

"But they're pretty things," the sergeant said. "Not what you'd have expected to appeal to a girl like her. But you never know. I'd like you to sign a statement that you identify them as your property."

"Very well," Sheila said.

"And, of course, you can dispose of them later as you see fit."

"I don't want them," Sheila repeated. "I don't want to see them again. Or the other things either, if you ever find them."

He had put the box back in his pocket. "I saw from the list you gave the police that a few things are missing. A gold locket, with a monogram on it in blue enamel, and a coral brooch. Possibly Teresa Swale sold them, though they must have been about the least valuable of the lot, and the locket, at least, would have been the easiest to identify."

I had been edging up to the table, and now I spoke.

"I was in Teresa Swale's room last Wednesday," I said. "Her landlady opened several of her drawers to show me how little Teresa had taken away with her. I saw a box in the top left-hand drawer of her chest of drawers that had some oddments of costume jewellery in it. There was a pair of pearl earrings the size of halfpennies in the box. Is that where you found these things?"

I suddenly had the whole of the attention of the man from Scotland Yard.

"The box was in the top left-hand drawer of the chest of drawers," he answered. "But, as it happens, there weren't any pearl earrings in it."

"When I saw the box," I said, "there were. But none of these things that you've just shown Mrs. Hill was there then."

"Her landlady says they were," the sergeant said.

"They weren't."

We looked at one another steadily.

At last he said, "I believe you want to return to London today, Miss Purvis. I think we can arrange that. And I think you'll probably be asked to repeat that statement when you get there by the officer in charge of the case."

CHAPTER FIFTEEN

Nicholas, the sergeant, and I travelled back to London together. We went by air and we were met at London Airport by a police car. I found this intimidating, and some reporters found it interesting. But our escort kept them at a distance and we settled down quietly in the car, just as we had in the aeroplane, to the delights and tribulations of gardening in Finchley.

To judge by the placards, the newspapers were full of the murder of Teresa Swale and, for the first time since I had heard of it on the Fenwicks' radio, I thought of Bernard and his story. He would never get his paper signed now. But did that matter any longer? *Alarum* would be jubilant at being the only paper in possession of the dead woman's own story. In fact, I had wasted a lot of time and effort trying to track her down. I ought to have stayed at home and quietly waited for her to turn up murdered.

But if I had done that, I should neither have met Nicholas nor learnt that when you are planting roses, the best thing to do is to put a dead crow under each bush. Specifically a crow, apparently.

I gave a start when I heard the sergeant say this, and thought that

157

I must have been dropping off to sleep. And perhaps I had. I have never been sure about this. I was very tired and I wanted to get away from all these policemen and be alone with Nicholas.

He gave no sign of wanting to be alone with me. In the aeroplane he had stared out at the country below us and hardly spoken. He seemed stunned by Sheila's certainty that it was he and not Roy who had married Teresa. Alec had not seemed nearly as worried by the way that Sheila had changed towards him. A less worrying sort of man, he had appeared confident that her cold anger against him for helping Nicholas in his deception would soon blow over.

The officer in charge of the case turned out to be a Superintendent Bolter, of whom, as I heard a little later from Janet, she had seen a good deal during the last twenty-four hours. The telephone number that I had left with Teresa's landlady had taken the police straight out to Hampstead, and Janet had already told them why I had gone to Teresa's room and then to Footfield and then to Edinburgh. But I had to tell this to Superintendent Bolter all over again, as well as to repeat to him my statement about what I had seen in Teresa's drawer.

When I had signed this statement, I was allowed to go home, but Nicholas had to stay on. I thought of waiting for him, but before I could suggest it, he told me that he would telephone later. His eyes met mine directly as he said it, and I realised that he did not want me to make any fuss just then. So I said I would expect his call; then I took a taxi back to Hampstead.

Janet clutched me and kissed me as if I had been away for a year. Bernard was much better, she told me, and if I liked, I could go to see him tomorrow. He would be home again in a few days. And *Alarum* was going to pay him for the story immediately. The Lincolns' troubles were over.

Though Janet did her best to remember from time to time that it was murder that had had this fortunate result and that there was something shocking about this, she could not conceal the lightening of her heart. But the more cheerful Janet became—chattering about the murder of Teresa Swale as if it were merely the climax of something that she had been following with impersonal interest in the newspapers—the more depressed I grew. I had a horrible feeling that some heavy responsibility rested on me and on me alone, yet I had not the faintest idea what it was, and I was too stupid, or too frightened, or too tired to be able to think. I listened halfheartedly to Janet as she talked on about the murder, about which she knew far more than I did. The most interesting thing she told me was that the police were not certain that Teresa had been killed in her room. This was something to do with the dust in the trunk, which was the wrong sort of dust for London. Besides this, the discovery of Teresa's body had been made because of complaints from other tenants in the house, and the state of the body by then was such that it was inexplicable why, if the body had been there for ten days, the complaints had not been made sooner.

"But if she was taken into the room only a day or two ago," Janet said, "it's more understandable, because it usually takes people a little while to work themselves up to make a complaint.

"How was she taken in?" I asked.

"Well, the murderer had her key, you see," Janet said. "Her handbag was there in the room, and it had her key in it along with all the other usual things, but she'd probably had it with her, wherever it was she was killed, so he could simply have let himself into the house when the coast was clear."

"How would he have known when the coast would be clear?" I asked. "The landlady lived in the room next door, and after all the questions that had been asked about Teresa, she'd have taken a good deal of interest in anything that went on in there."

"Yes, but wet or fine, at seven-thirty sharp every evening, the landlady went along the road to a café and ate fish and chips. Then she went on a bit farther to a pub and stayed there till closing time. So the murderer could have slipped in any time in the evening."

"Only you can't just slip into a house, carrying a corpse over your arm like an overcoat," I said.

"No, I suppose it was in another trunk, or something," Janet said.

An image of Callie and Lance rose before me. I could see them doing the murder, putting the body in a trunk, and carrying it into

Teresa's room at some odd moment when the coast was clear. They would have the ruthlessness and the crazy daring. Yet I still believed that when they had questioned me, up on the moor, they had not known where Teresa was.

I began to think about Teresa's landlady and to wonder if she could have been involved. I wondered why she had lied about Sheila's bits of jewellery. I knew that when I had seen the cardboard box in the drawer, the topaz pendant, the garnet brooch, and the opal ring had not been in it. I could not have missed them amongst the plastic beads and the glittering glass. And there was also the puzzle of the big pearl earrings which had gone missing.

Perhaps, I thought, it would be a good idea to talk to the old woman again. Perhaps, when Nicholas had telephoned, that was what I would do.

But Nicholas did not telephone until the evening, so the rest of the day passed without my doing anything but having a bath and washing some of my clothes. By the time that he telephoned I had given up the hope that he was going to and I was in a state of feverish tension that I did not want Janet to see. I did not want her to guess that I was passing the time thinking out all the dire things that could have happened to him since I had seen him last. He could have been arrested for the murder of Teresa Swale. He could have been arrested for the murder of David Hill. He could have been murdered himself. He could have committed suicide. He could have decided that he did not like me.

The sound of his voice on the telephone had the effect of strong spirits on my complaining nervous system. Wildly excited, I took for granted that I should be going straight out to meet him somewhere. But that was not what Nicholas had in mind.

"Elspeth, I thought you'd want to know this," he said. "Roy didn't leave from Prestwick last night."

His voice was curt and he sounded in a hurry. My excitement began to ebb.

"How do you know?" I asked. "Have you heard from him?"

"No, Bolter told me," he said. "They were watching for him there, but he never turned up. Bolter asked me if I knew anything about it."

"But Roy can't have had anything to do with Teresa's murder," I said. "You said that yourself. You said that if she'd been dead for at least a week, he couldn't have been in the country when she was killed."

"It isn't because of Teresa's murder that the police want him," Nicholas said. "It's to sort out that business about which of us married her. And about that, Elspeth . . ." He paused. "I've done a lot of thinking about it today. I suppose the truth can still be proved, whatever Roy decides to say, because apart from my passport, I think I can probably find somebody in Rome who'll remember I was around about the date of the marriage, and the police can probably dig up the registrar and the witnesses, and there'll be Roy's signature, too. Even if he used my name and a fair imitation of my handwriting, it ought to be possible to prove it's a forgery. But that's all going to take time, and so I've been thinking . . ."

As he hesitated again, I said, "I shouldn't worry about its taking time. Sheila will come round when she's had time to think about it. It was a bad shock she had yesterday, but she'll get over it."

"Elspeth darling, I'm not thinking about Sheila; I'm thinking about you," he said, "and that it isn't going to be possible for me to act like a human being till this whole damned thing's cleared up."

"But I believe you——" I began.

As I said it, some remnants of doubt, which had lain like a dark sediment at the bottom of my mind, seemed to dissolve and leave everything clear. But Nicholas did not let me finish.

He went on. "I told you, I've done a lot of thinking about it all, and I've realised there's one person who must know all about it. So I'm going to see her tomorrow evening. I can't go till the evening, as I've a day's work to do. But as soon as I've seen her, I'll telephone again. Good night now, and stop worrying about it all."

Before I could say anything more, he rang off. I wished that he had not been in such a hurry, but all the same I was feeling happier than I could remember ever having felt in my life. I went on holding the telephone for a moment with a kind of tenderness, as if it were a physical link with Nicholas; then I put it down and, as I did so, saw Janet watching me from the doorway.

"Well, don't say good never comes out of evil," she said, and went out again, understandingly leaving me to myself.

I knew that it was Mrs. Bullock whom Nicholas was going to see. I did not hope much from this, because I did not think it likely that she would admit knowing anything that could conceivably do harm to her son. But this did not worry me, because I had meant what I had said when I had told Nicholas not to worry about the matter's taking some time to unravel. What was a little time, less or more? But I suppose if he had taken up that attitude himself, I should not have achieved quite the serenity, the calm certainty about the future, that I did for most of the rest of the evening.

Anxiety crept back again later, though I did not know quite why. I went to bed early, but slept restlessly. As I was going to bed, an odd idea had occurred to me, and though at first I did not take it seriously, it kept coming back, waking me up and forcing me to think about it. I got up earlier than usual, went out to the kitchen and made tea. Janet heard me moving about and called out to me.

When I took her a cup of tea, she said, "You know, I think it would be a good idea if you went to see Bernard today, instead of me."

"He'd far sooner see you," I answered.

"Oh no, he's mad with curiosity about everything that's been happening, and you can tell him much more than I can," she said.

"All right," I said, but I was thinking about something else, deciding that there was something I would do before I went to see Bernard.

I did not tell Janet anything about it, because she seemed glad to think that my connection with the case of Teresa Swale was practically at an end, and when she asked me, as I set out after breakfast, why I was going out so early, when there was no chance that I should be let in to see Bernard for another couple of hours, I told her that I wanted to do some shopping.

In fact, I did do some shopping. I went to a Woolworth's and bought a pair of enormous pearl earrings. After that, I got on a bus to Tottenham Court Road, changed there and got on another to Theobald's Road, then walked to Teresa's lodging.

When I rang, the landlady came to the door. But she opened it only a crack. I could see one of her eyes peering out at me. After a moment, she opened the door a little further and thrust out the big head on the twisted old neck.

"Listen, my duck, if you know what's good for you, you'll keep away from here," she said. "It's nothing but coppers and reporters in and out all day. That's nothing for a nice girl like you to get mixed up in."

I brought the earrings out of my pocket and held them out where she could see them.

She began to look frightened. Giving a furtive glance behind her, as if she were afraid someone might be listening, she leant further out of the door and said in a croaking whisper, "I never touched nothing. You can't say I did. A locket, they kept saying—a gold locket with blue letters—and a coral brooch. They as good as said I'd taken them. Me—what that poor girl trusted as if I was her mother. I'd never touch nothing what didn't belong to me, I said; I've never even seen them, I said; and what's more, I said, what would I be wanting with things like that?"

"I know," I said. "Old-fashioned things. But something smart like these earrings. . . ." I went a little nearer to the door. "I expect Teresa would have liked you to have them, and I shouldn't dream of trying to deprive you of anything which was practically a gift from her—her last gift. But if you'd consider exchanging them for this pair I've brought you, which I think are exactly the same, you can't think how grateful I'd be."

Lines of deep thought furrowed her yellow old face.

"If they're exactly the same, what's the difference to you?" she asked.

I did not answer.

Suddenly she plunged a hand into one of the deep pockets in her flowered overall, groped there amongst dirty handkerchiefs and torn scraps of paper, and started to bring something out.

That was all I had wanted. I had wanted to make sure that she had taken the earrings. A straight question would only have met denials, but, as I had hoped, I had puzzled her into giving herself away.

When her hand went deep down into the pocket again and came out empty, it did not worry me.

"No, my duck," she said, "I don't know what you're talking about. I took care of that poor girl as if she was my own, and I don't know anything about pearl earrings, and if I did, I'd never have touched them, any more than you would yourself."

The door closed in my face.

Later I told this story to Bernard. I told him everything else besides that I could remember about the last hectic few days, and as he lay and listened in his hospital bed, he showed none of the signs of being horrified that Janet had predicted. As she ought to have known, he did not horrify easily. It was interest and enthusiasm that lit up his grey, drained face, and he gave me his crooked, affectionate smile.

"You're going into the wrong job, Elspeth," he said. "Teaching's a static sort of life. You have to stay in one place for weeks on end."

"And how I'm looking forward to it!" I said sincerely. "Detecting is something I've got out of my system for good."

Both of us were speaking in low voices. He was in a small ward, with only three other people in it, but we did not want to be overheard, even by them.

"Only you haven't quite finished the job in hand, have you?" Bernard said. "That's why you're here now."

"I'm here strictly on a visit to the sick," I said, "to cheer you up a little."

"Well, cheer me up a bit more and explain that experiment with the earrings," he said. "Why does it matter whether or not the landlady took them? What does it tell you, except that, like most of us, she isn't quite the noble character she makes herself out to be?"

"What I think it tells us," I said, hitching my chair closer to him, "is that the old woman didn't know anything about Sheila Hill's

164

jewellery being in that drawer until the police started questioning her about it. I don't think she's the person who put it there. I think that after she'd shown me the earrings and tried them on herself, as she did when I was there, and decided she fancied herself in them, she went back and took them, really only borrowing them and meaning to put them back before Teresa got home. If she'd borrowed the other things in the same way before I came, I don't think she'd ever have let me look into the drawer, in case, in some mysterious way, I knew something about them. And when the police asked her about the jewellery, she was taken by surprise and said it had been there all along only to show how honest she was, because she'd a guilty conscience about the earrings."

"So the murderer put the jewellery there, when he was dumping Teresa's body," Bernard said.

"It looks like it, doesn't it?"

"Only you see what that means, don't you? It means Teresa didn't steal it in the first place." He frowned up at the white ceiling. "You know, Elspeth, from the way you told me the whole story, I thought I knew whom you suspected. But that person wouldn't ever steal a handful of jewellery. No . . . Unless . . ." He looked back at me with one eyebrow cocked. "Was that jewellery given to Sheila Hill by her husband?"

"Yes," I said.

"So in sheer jealousy, perhaps . . . An if the motive for David's murder was hatred, plain hatred, exaggerated by Sheila's feeling that she oughtn't to marry again because of the boy. . . . You know, in the end one always has to come back to the fact that except when it's a sadistic murder, there's no motive for killing a young child like that except that it's in the way. And even if David was in Fenwick's way or to some extent in Nicholas Hill's, he was more in Teresa's than anyone else's, or so she thought, didn't she?"

"No," I said. "She didn't think David was in her way. Long before the murder, she'd found out that the man she was married to wasn't Nicholas Hill. There were photographs of Nicholas in the house—Mrs. Fenwick told me so. And Teresa'd certainly have heard quite soon after she got to the house whom they were photographs of. So that really does away with that particular motive of hers."

"Yes, and if she'd done the murder, would she ever have made the mistake about the chair?" Bernard said, "She, of all people, knew about the child's pulling the chair out of his mother's room to climb on to, to try to reach the flowers at the window; so surely she'd have remembered to put it there herself. But if he was in someone else's way. . . . The trouble is, though, I haven't met any of the people. I don't know what I'd feel myself about the way they might be capable of acting. But Fenwick couldn't have stolen that jewellery for its own sake, could he? Still, it might actually have been stolen as a blind, to help cast suspicion on Teresa, the person in the household whom they all knew the least about. Yet it seems not to have been planted on her until she was dead."

"I'm sure it wasn't," I said.

"Because there wasn't an opportunity before? Because it turned out not to be necessary? Yet it's just the sort of thing which might have got her convicted. The thing that would have turned the scale. Not logical, of course, but what jury's logical? And there's still the question of the two missing pieces, the locket and the coral brooch. As you said, probably the least valuable and most easily recognisable of the lot; so why were they got rid of? And there's also the problem of why Teresa's body was returned to her room. Why wasn't it dumped in a pond or a river? And how was it jammed into that trunk so long after she was dead, if that's what happened? I don't believe that would have been easy."

"Yes—how and why?"

"Because——" Bernard began, then stopped and eyed me curiously. "You've made up your own mind about that, haven't you, Elspeth?"

I felt a sudden uneasiness. He was looking too interested, too eager for someone who also looked so frail that the mere warmth of such interest might burn up what was left of him.

"Not really," I said. "And anyway, it's nothing to do with me. And I've kept you talking long enough."

I stood up.

Bernard gave an impatient frown. "Sit down. The body was meant to be found; that's the answer. Not only found, but identified. Quickly. By someone who thought that would give him an alibi."

"I expect you're right," I said, trying to sound as if I did not much care whether he was or not, or what the answer might be.

Bernard gave a laugh as he looked up at me. I had not deceived him at all. We had always understood each other too well for that ever to be easy.

Yet I was not going to admit this, or let him go on with the discussion just then.

"I expect Janet will be coming along to see you later in the day," I said, "and perhaps they'll tell her when they're going to let you come home. We can thrash the rest of this out then."

I stooped and kissed him.

"Elspeth, you're up to something," he said. "And I wouldn't dream of trying to stop you, because I happen to know you wouldn't take any notice. So I'll just say—please be careful. I mean it. Be careful."

His squinting gaze was unusually serious as I turned and left him.

CHAPTER SIXTEEN

I thought Bernard had been wrong at one point. He had said that there could be no reason for killing a young child like David Hill except that he was in the way. I could think of at least one other reason.

I believe I had thought of it first while I was soaking dreamily in the bath at Hunter Law and had seen the plaster cupid in the ceiling leering knowingly down at me, as if it had something to tell me. To tell—that was the point. Not that I had guessed then what it had to tell. But now I knew. Or I thought that I knew. What I did not know was what to do about it.

One possibility was to do nothing and wait for the police to find the thing out for themselves, if they had not done so already. Another possibility was to go to see Superintendent Bolter and tell him what I thought I knew. Still another was to wait until Nicholas telephoned me in the evening from Footfield, after seeing Mrs. Bullock. But there was something about each of those possibilities, particularly the last, that I did not like. In the end, after I had had lunch in a Lyon's and turned the problem over and over in my mind until it had come to a standstill, I decided to telephone Superintendent Bolter.

I am glad now to remember that I had that much sense. It makes me feel that I have some of the instincts of a responsible person. At the same time, I know that when I was told that the superintendent was not available, I was relieved and I said very hastily that the matter wasn't urgent and that I did not want to speak to anyone else instead of him. It could wait, I said.

What I meant was that it could wait until I had been to Footfield, and, as I said it, I realised that I had really meant all along to go to see Mrs. Bullock before Nicholas could do so.

From Paddington Station I telephoned Janet that I should not be home again until fairly late in the evening, but I did not tell her where I was going. Bernard, of course, had guessed what I would do, but it was unlikely that he would tell her. I caught an afternoon train and settled down in it to work out exactly what I wanted to say to Mrs. Bullock. A fellow passenger, seeing me staring into space, insisted on lending me a newspaper. I took it with thanks, opened it at random, and, holding it up as a screen, went on plotting my course of action behind it. As I never turned a page, I must have appeared to have an obsessive interest, probably unusual at my age, in stocks and shares.

All the way to Footfield, first in the train to Gloucester and then in the bus that dropped me at the Rose and Thorn, I felt as if so much had happened since my earlier visit, so much ground had been covered, that I should find that all sorts of changes had come about in the village since I had seen it last. The leaves on the trees might have turned to gold, or even fallen. The flowers in the gardens would surely all be different.

But as I stepped off the bus and started to walk along the single street, I saw that the sweet peas and the gladioli were blooming where I had left them. A cat that I had seen on a doorstep, washing itself, seemed just to be finishing the toilet that on that other visit it had interrupted for a moment to watch me pass. There was an uncanny sense of repetition about everything and, as I took the turning by the church, passed Footfield House, and went up to Mrs. Bullock's door, I felt as if the other visit had been only a sort of rehearsal for this, the real performance.

As soon as Mrs. Bullock opened the door, the feeling of recognition vanished, although she was wearing the same white cotton dress with black spots, with her grey hair bound in the same iron plaits across the top of her head. On her face, as she looked at me, there was an expression quite unlike the one that had been there before. She made no movement to invite me in. If it had been by her son's instructions that she had done so before, it was plain that she had no such instructions now.

I said, "How do you do, Mrs. Bullock? I'm sorry to trouble you again, but I believe you've got the keys of Footfield House."

It was not what she had been expecting, and uncertainty clouded her gaze.

I went on. "Of course, you've read the news about Teresa Swale and you'll have heard from your son what my interest in her was. I saw him in Scotland, you know."

"Why should you think I've heard from him?" she said. "He's left for America."

"Has he?" I said. "I just thought he might have telephoned before he left. Even so, I suppose he mightn't have said anything about me. I was trying to trace Teresa Swale, you know, to get her to sign a paper for my brother-in-law, so that he could publish a story he'd written about her. He was in hospital—he still is—so he couldn't do it himself. And now, of course, he doesn't need the signature. But he thinks it would help the story if he could add a little firsthand description of the interior of Footfield House. He can't come himself, so he sent me again. And I remember seeing Mr. Fenwick bring you the keys the other evening, and I thought if you would be so very kind as to let me borrow them——"

"I couldn't do that," she interrupted flatly.

"Oh please, just for a very little while," I said.

"I've no right to let you have them," she said.

"I'm sure Mrs. Hill wouldn't mind."

"I'm sure she would. But, as it happens, the house doesn't belong to her any more."

"Have the new people moved in, then?" I asked.

"There's nobody going to move in for a long time," she said. "They're going to pull it apart and turn it into a country club."

"Then there's no one who could possibly mind if I went in, just for a peep," I said. "If you don't like the idea of me going in on my own, perhaps you'd come with me. Only that'd be more trouble for you than letting me borrow the keys." I paused, turning to look towards the house next door. "Actually, with an old house like that, that's been standing empty for so long, there's probably a broken pane somewhere. I expect I can get in quite easily without troubling you at all."

I took a step towards her gate.

She came swiftly after me.

"No, don't you do that," she said. "That'd be trespassing. Just wait a minute and I'll come with you. Wait while I get the key. I don't suppose I ought but, as you say, it can't do any harm."

She turned back into her cottage, emerging again a moment later with a key in her hand. But she was frowning and full of suspicion as we walked along the road towards the tumble-down gate of Foot-field House.

Unlocking the front door, she led the way into the house.

Almost like a wave washing over me, the sense of the dreadful sadness of the place engulfed me. I suppose it was not really in the house, but waiting in my own mind to be released by the musty smell of disuse, the sight of the dust on the fine old floors, of the cobwebs cloaking the windows, and the corners of the gracefully curving stair.

I stood still, looking round, while my heart raced.

Mrs. Bullock went to the foot of the staircase.

"Well, if you want to see where it happened," she said in her flat, dull voice, "it was up here."

Then, as I did not move, but only went on looking about me, she said more sharply, "That *is* what you want, isn't it—to see the window where she did it?"

"Really I just want to get the atmosphere of the place," I said. "The more I can see, the better. And that window—yes, of course."

I started up the staircase, going quickly, so that I reached the top when Mrs. Bullock, treading heavily and holding onto the bannisters, was only halfway up. Before she reached my side, I had had time to look along the broad passage, shadowy because of the way that its one window was overhung outside by the clematis, and to see what I was really looking for.

This was a door that had a key in its keyhole. That it was the door of the room that had been Sheila's bedroom had a certain rightness about it. As Mrs. Bullock joined me, I walked purposefully to this door, thrust it open, and stood staring in.

She hurried to my side to see what I was staring at. I took a quick step behind her, thrust at her stiff back with all my strength and, as she went heavily staggering into the room, I slammed the door on her and locked it. Then as she started to shout and pound on the door, I ran down the stairs and out into the garden and back to her cottage.

I did not know how long I had for what I wanted to do. I did not know whether or not Mrs. Bullock's shouts could be heard. The room into which I had locked her was at the back of the house, overlooking the big garden, so there was a chance that even if she screamed her loudest, no one would hear her. On the other hand, there might be some cottage nearer than I knew. So it was best to waste as little time as possibile.

Not that I was in a mood to waste time. The danger was that, in my nervous haste, I might be less thorough than was needed, and would hurry and make a muddle. Realising this, I stood still in the little sitting room and tried to think. Where should I start? In the bedroom, obviously. I found the staircase, shut away behind what looked like a cupboard door, and rushed up to the tiny, neat bedroom.

I left it in chaos, ashamed of the sight and thinking that I would come back and tidy up later, if I had time. But I had not found what I was looking for. The even smaller spare bedroom also yielded nothing. So did the bathroom and, by the time that I had finished with it, all the excitement with which I had started had ebbed, and I was in a state of cold, despondent fright. How on earth was I going to explain my actions if in the end I found nothing? Should I perhaps have to plead insanity, and might that plea be not quite as much of a fiction as I wanted to think?

I was shivering and there were tears of fear and frustration in my eyes when at last, rolled up in a pair of cotton stockings in a basket of mending in the sitting room, I found Sheila Hill's gold locket and coral brooch.

As I saw them come tumbling out of the folds of the stockings into my hand, I felt the complete disbelief that one sometimes does when something on which one's whole mind has been concentrated suddenly comes to pass. Even though I could feel the locket and the brooch, cold and unexpectedly heavy, in the palm of my hand, I had the feeling that there was some trick about it, some illusion. But at the sound of a key in the latch, my fingers closed convulsively. Panting, as the door from the street opened, I swung round to face Mrs. Bullock.

It was not Mrs. Bullock who came in. It was her son, and as I met his light grey eyes across the small, disordered room, I knew the worst fear that I had ever felt in my life. It was worse than I had felt in the car with Callie and Lance. But as he came inside and quietly closed the door behind him, I sensed that I was making a mistake. There was nothing in Roy's face to fear, unless it was his own fear which gave that blind stare to his eyes. It was not a cruel face, or a murderous one.

He leant against the door and said wretchedly, "So she didn't hand them all over to me after all, though she swore she had. And now she's done for herself, hasn't she?"

I opened my fingers and let him see what lay on my palm.

"Yes," he said, "she's done for. And for a couple of things like that. . . . Where is she, Elspeth?"

"I locked her up in one of the bedrooms at Footfield House," I said. "I think—I think it was Sheila's bedroom. The one from which your mother was stealing some bits of jewellery when David saw her and said he'd tell his mother."

He nodded again. "Poor mother," he said. "She'd always had so little. She couldn't bear it when Sheila came home and took over the house. She always hated Sheila."

"Oughtn't we to be saying—poor David?" I said. I thought for a moment and added, "And poor Roy. Poor everybody."

"You needn't be sorry for me," he said. "I'll get by. I always have. But mother's done for. And all because of that damned jewellery. I didn't even know she liked the stuff. I could have sent her . . . But not when she took it, of course. No . . ." He brushed a hand confusedly across his forehead. "I'd nothing then."

"How long have you known she murdered David?" I asked.

"Since—oh, since it happened, of course. But I didn't know about Teresa until—the night before last, wasn't it? No, the one before that. The night you and Nick went up to Scotland. I got you out of the way and came down here, because mother'd told me she'd got Teresa here. She didn't tell me—till I got here—that she was dead." He closed his eyes for a moment. "How did you find out about the kid?"

"For one thing," I said, "she was the one person who lied about David's habit of climbing up to the window. She said he never did it, but we knew he did. So it looked as if she wanted to make things as black as possible for Teresa."

"Of course," Roy said. "She couldn't bear Teresa."

"And you took Teresa's body back to her room so that she'd be found and identified while it was still possible to say how long she'd been dead, because you'd be able to show you hadn't been in the country then."

"Of course."

"You'll still be an accessory after the fact," I said.

He gave me a bewildered look, as if he didn't know what the words meant. Then he gave me a quite sweet smile.

"It isn't murder, and I'll get away with it," he said. "You needn't worry about me, Elspeth."

The curious thing was that I was worrying about him. I could not help it.

"How did you manage to put Teresa into the trunk, when she'd been dead for so long?" I asked. "Taking her into the house—that was a frightful risk."

"There were two trunks," he said. "Reggie'd had them in the Sudan. They were just the same and they'd both got his initials on them. Mother had one of them here, and when she killed Teresa, she put her into it straight away, then cabled me to come home." He made a choking sound. "She thought I'd be pleased, you know. She thought all Teresa's death would mean to me was that I could come home. I shouldn't have to go on hiding from her. And what it really means is that I've got to go into hiding again, give up everything—oh God, God!" He drummed against the door behind him with his fists. "What's going to happen to me?"

I could not think of anything to say. I could not even say anything about the child who had had all taken from him simply because he was just old enough to speak a few words. Enough words to betray the trusted housekeeper.

I wondered how far Mrs. Bullock had betrayed that trust before David Hill, going to fetch the chair to climb on from his mother's bedroom, had caught Mrs. Bullock at his mother's jewel case and, certainly not understanding in the least what was happening, had said, perhaps, "That's Mummy's."

How much had Mrs. Bullock pillaged Reggie Hill's sick mother and Reggie himself during the time that he had been abroad? That was a question to which there would never be any answer.

But there was one question which was important and to which I wanted the answer.

"I still don't understand, Roy; why did your mother kill Teresa?" I said. "I suppose Teresa could have got money out of you—perhaps a lot of money—because you'd have gone through a bad time if it had come out that you were the husband of a woman like her. But

175

she couldn't have involved you in the murder itself, because you weren't there and you hadn't a shadow of a motive."

"Oh, don't you understand? Mother was wearing one of those damned things—she felt so safe, she was *wearing* it—that opal ring—when she opened the door to Teresa, and of course Teresa knew it and realised who'd been behind what she'd gone through. And mother waited for her chance and then brought the poker down on Teresa's head." He gave an angry, sobbing laugh. "An opal ring; a coral brooch! I tell you, if it had been diamonds . . ."

He stopped abruptly. A car had just stopped outside the cottage.

It was Nicholas. I recognised the sound of his step in the road before he reached the door. So did Roy, and I saw him tense himself as he turned, when Nicholas rang, to open the door.

I cried out a warning to Nicholas. Then I felt foolish, because nothing happened. Nothing violent. Nothing frightening. The two of them merely looked at one another and I saw again that air of understanding between them in which friendship and enmity were so mingled that in the end it was impossible to tell which was which.

Then Roy held his hand out.

"Let me have your car key, Nick," he said. "I came by bus, but I'd sooner leave another way."

"Why did you come at all?" Nick said. "You know they're looking for you to sort out that marriage business."

"That's why I couldn't get away," Roy said. "That was your doing, Nick—although you swore to me once you'd never tell anyone about that marriage."

"I never swore that," Nicholas said. "I said I'd cover up for you, if I could. That didn't mean shouldering the load of your lunacy for the rest of my life."

"So far as I'm concerned, a promise is a promise," Roy said austerely.

"So far as you're concerned, a promise doesn't mean a damned thing and never has," Nicholas answered. "And you still haven't told me—why did you come here?"

"I didn't know where else to go," Roy answered with the note of childish helplessness in his voice that I had heard once or twice before. "I knew you wouldn't help me this time, so I thought of mother. But that's no good now. Ask Elspeth. So let me have your car, Nick."

There was a silence; then Nicholas handed over his car key.

Roy responded with a forced grin of almost frenzied cheerfulness, clapped Nicholas on the shoulder, and, as he went out, cried, "Thanks—and don't worry; you'll get it back."

We heard the car drive away.

As it did so, some fury that Nicholas had managed to hold back while he was face to face with Roy got out of control and exploded over me.

"You damned, crazy, interfering, little fool; what the hell d'you think you're doing here?" he shouted at me. "Didn't I tell you I'd ring up after I'd been here? Couldn't you wait?"

"But I knew she was a murderess and you didn't," I said. "You wouldn't have been on the lookout, and she might have done anything!"

I said quite a lot else. But I had to repeat it all later, because at that point Nicholas gathered me into his arms.

And that is almost the whole of the story, since there is no need for me to describe the trial and conviction of Mrs. Bullock. But perhaps I should add that I like teaching much better than I had expected. For one thing, I seem to be better at it than I had expected. I am perhaps a little short on discipline, but I am told that I make up for it by my imaginative approach to the subject, which the more intelligent pupil finds stimulating. I hope she really does, poor thing. I certainly try to do my best for her.

I am lucky, I suppose, in not having to worry about how long I am going to go on liking the job. I might keep it up for a time after Nicholas and I get married, but I have not made up my mind about that yet. Janet says I am a fool even to think of it, but then, for the present, she cannot imagine any kind of life which does not consist of adoring an infant daughter. She and Bernard are looking for a small house in the suburbs and seem to be reasonably free of financial worries. Bernard is writing the life story of a woman who produced nine children in four years. She needs the money *Alarum* is ready to pay her as badly as Teresa Swale ever did, and she is less likely to disappear suddenly.

I wish I could stop thinking about Teresa. She was innocent of almost everything of which she was suspected. She did not murder David. She did not steal Sheila's jewellery. She did not try to blackmail anybody except the husband who had deserted her and who owed her all that she could have asked and more. Yet there was something about her which made it easy for that horrible woman, Mrs. Bullock, to use her as a cloak for her own evil. That quality, whatever it was, was what I had heard in Teresa's voice on Bernard's tape recorder, and which prejudiced me against her, as it had everyone else. I think of it as the voice of the born victim—the person whose fate it is to draw out the worst in everyone else.

There is another problem that comes to my mind a little too often for comfort—the problem of Billie Bullock.

Nicholas refuses now to blame him for anything. He says that with a mother like he had, he never had a chance and it is a wonder that he did not turn into a perfect monster, and in Nicholas's memory they are friends again, and nothing but friends. When his car was found, with the note in it, by the sea shore, with the footprints leading down to a line of angry breakers, he went silent and miserable for days. And, of course, Roy Carney is dead. There can be no question about that. His public and his publishers mourn him, as well as Nicholas.

But I view the matter rather differently. For when I think of that suicide note, which was written rather in the "think-of-me-at-my-best" style, which I do not find wholly convincing, and when I remember Roy's certainty, at our last meeting, that he would get by, because he always had, I sometimes wonder if Billie Bullock is as dead as Roy Carney.

I have a feeling that some day, when I am on a railway journey— for instance, the long journey to Edinburgh, when Nicholas and I go to stay with Mrs. Fenwick, as we have arranged to do next summer, since Alec and Sheila live mostly in London now that they are married and the old lady feels rather lonely—well, I have a feeling that on such a journey, when I have bought a thriller at the station, by a new writer who has been rapidly acquiring fame, I shall find myself reading about the adventures of a woman called Nastasia Popova, or Li Cho Sun, or some such thing, and somehow know that I have come face to face with the reincarnated spirit of Leni Briefback.

9 781471 907104